Thomas. tr Steele

An Eastern Love-Story

Kusa jakaya, a Buddhistic legend

Thomas. tr Steele

An Eastern Love-Story
Kusa jakaya, a Buddhistic legend

ISBN/EAN: 9783337244651

Printed in Europe, USA, Canada, Australia, Japan

Cover: Foto ©Andreas Hilbeck / pixelio.de

More available books at **www.hansebooks.com**

KUSA JATAKAYA.

An Eastern Love-Story.

KUSA JĀTAKAYA,

A BUDDHISTIC LEGEND:

RENDERED, FOR THE FIRST TIME, INTO ENGLISH VERSE,

FROM THE

SINHALESE POEM OF

ALAGIYAVANNA MOHOTTĀLA,

BY

THOMAS STEELE,

CEYLON CIVIL SERVICE.

LONDON:

TRÜBNER & CO., 60 PATERNOSTER ROW.

1871.

Inscribed,

With Much Love,

to

C. R. S.,

At Whose Request the Translation

Was Written,

Six Happy Years Ago.

PREFACE.

BUDDHISTS believe that their Great Teacher, GAUTAMA
BUDDHA, while a Bōdisat, before attaining to Buddha-
hood, underwent, as they hold do *all* sentient beings,
countless transmigrations, five hundred and fifty of which
he afterwards revealed to his followers. These are con-
tained in the PANSIYAPANAS JĀTAKAPOTA, or *Book of the
Five Hundred and Fifty Births*, a prose classic translated
from the ancient Buddhistic legends in the Pāli language into the vernacular tongue early in the fourteenth
century, during the reign of PRĀKKRAMA BĀHU IV., King
of CEYLON. The probable date of the Pāli legends cannot be ascertained ; but there can be no question they
are of remote antiquity.

In one of these transmigrations, the Bōdisat was born
as KUSA, Emperor of Dambadiva or Jambudwīpa (INDIA);
and his adventures, while in that life, form the subject
of the KUSA JĀTAKAYA, a favourite legendary poem of
high repute among the Sinhalese, of which a rendering
into English verse is now for the first time submitted to
the reader. The original poem, founded on the prose
legend in *The Book of the Five Hundred and Fifty Births*,
was written, as the concluding stanza shows, in 1610
A.D., by ALAGIYAVANNA MOHOTṬĀLA, Secretary or Writer
to the Household of a native chieftain of high rank.

ALAGIYAVANNA is regarded as one of the most distinguished poets of Ceylon by his countrymen, among

whom, though the circumstance may perhaps cause sur-
prise to many English readers, poetry has, from remote
times, been an object of earnest study and liking. Of
the KUSA JĀTAKAYA it has been said, "The unity of its
plan, the steady progress of its narrative, and a certain
unaffected display of genuine feeling, . . . entitle it to
rank as a poem of the highest merit."* Although this
measure of praise should, perhaps, be qualified, the Legend
is undeniably a favourable specimen of Sinhalese poetry;
and I am fain to hope that the version now offered may
be of interest to Englishmen, as evidence of a vein of
Oriental literature almost wholly unsuspected at home,
as illustrating Buddhistic history, precept, and practice,
and modes of life and feeling in the East, little known
here, and as showing what engaged the thoughts of at
least one builder of "the lofty rhyme" in Ceylon, at the
time when SHAKSPEARE, resting from his dramatic
labours, was enjoying a happy but too short afternoon
of life at Stratford, and RALEIGH consoled his captivity
in The Tower with gorgeous day-dreams, never to be
realised, of golden realms he believed himself destined to
discover beyond the Spanish Main.

The Legend is a love-story, and exhibits in many places
great beauty and tenderness of sentiment. The student
of Comparative Mythology, and the lover of old-world
stories, will be interested in finding ancient Aryan
incidents, which appear in the *Mahabharata*, here worked

---

* ALWIS's *Introduction to the Sidat Sangarāva*, a scholarly and
highly interesting book. Mr ALWIS is at present engaged on
another important work, *The Descriptive Catalogue of Sinhalese
Authors*, undertaken at the request of the Governor, SIR HERCULES
ROBINSON, whose enlightened action in regard to Sinhalese literature and antiquities calls for very cordial recognition.

up into a Buddhistic myth, in a country where an almost exact counterpart of the Judgment of SOLOMON,* but *not* derived from Hebrew sources, has long been current. The seven kings who are to marry one bride; the hero disguised as a potter, a groom, and a cook; the miraculous birth of the hero by the favour of INDRA; and many minor incidents of the poem, reveal a close connection between the Legend and the old Sanskrit epic, and, it may be added, between both and many popular tales of Western Europe.

The translation reads stanza for stanza with the original, which consists of six hundred and eighty-seven stanzas of four lines each, all four rhyming alike, with, not unfrequently, double rhymes in the middle of the lines. The translation is in many places necessarily freer. Old Ballad Measure has been chosen as the one best adapted to convey the spirit of the original, and as affording room for amplifying, where necessary, into English verse, the remarkable compression which occasionally distinguishes Sinhalese poetry. I have been urged to publish the original text in Roman characters, side by side with the English version, as was done by TURNOUR in his translation of the *Mahavansö*. This would be easy, as ancient Sinhalese poetry contains none of the aspirated letters frequent in prose, and, to a certain extent, difficult to express by Roman characters; but I refrain, for the present at least, from adopting the suggestion. It may, perhaps, be carried into effect hereafter, should this venture meet with favour enough to warrant a second edition.

A few specimens of Sinhalese epigrams and stories have been appended at the end of the volume, in the hope that

* See Note to stanza 316, p. 218.

they may prove not unattractive to readers who take interest in Aryan folk-lore, that oldest, and, in some respects, most inviting body of unwritten history. The resemblances to old stories common in the West will not escape remark.

The works, to which grateful acknowledgment should here be made, consulted in preparing the Notes, were the following :—HARDY's *Eastern Monachism and Manual of Buddhism ;* SCHLAGINTWEIT's *Buddhism in Tibet ;* HODGSON's *Literature and Religion of Buddhists;* MAX MÜLLER's *Essays on Comparative Mythology;* ALWIS's *Introduction to the Sidat Sangarāva ;* SKEEN's *Adam's Peak ;* COLONEL FORBES's *Eleven Years in Ceylon ;* MACREADY's *The Sela's Message;* A. M. FERGUSON's *Souvenirs of Ceylon;* CLOUGH's *Sinhalese Dictionary ;* WARD's *Literature and Religion of the Hindus ;* PERCIVAL's *Land of the Vedas ;* TORRENS' *Travels in Ladak and Kashmir ;* CAPPER's *Duke of Edinburgh in Ceylon;* FERGUSSON's *History of Architecture, and Tree and Serpent Worship;* Sir J. LUBBOCK's *Origin of Civilisation ;* GLADSTONE's *Homer and the Homeric Age ;* COX's *Tales of the Gods and Heroes.*

The original poem, it may be added, is one of the books prescribed in Ceylon by the Board of Examiners for the Civil Service.   T. S.

WALTON, *May* 27, 1871.

In looking for the origin of Western myths it is better to go as far back as possible & not begin far from the source in Versified versions of Versified versions. CONTENTS. *I would rather gather oral Traditions, anywhere*

EPIGRAMS.

STORIES.

These stories were gathered for
me. S.F.L. I have a great
many more but many of
them are not fit for printing.
They are coarse & dirty

KUSA JĀTAKĒ:

A BUDDHISTIC LEGEND IN VERSE.

—◇—

PART I.

Proem.

——

1

The Ascription of Worship.

HIM who, a Sun, through Unbelief's thick, gloomy darkness breaks,
Who beams on faithful hearts as beams the Moon on
   lotus lakes,
With virtue stored as is the Main with precious jewels
   strown,
Him of three worlds Chief Teacher, shall I adoring own !

2

Him who, all lusts uprooting through long-continued
   strife,
Became the BUDDHA, and proclaimed the bliss of
   heavenly life !

A

The true and precious DOCTRINE which through the
    world was shown
By him, shall I unceasingly with adoration own !

3

The PRIESTHOOD, that has blessings shed upon this
    world of ours,
That set its sacred feet, which are as budding lotus
    flowers,
Upon the heads of Brahmans, of gods and men—alone
A field of merit, fount* of worth, shall I adoring own !

4

The Invocation.

May seven-armed* MAHA BRAHMA, may VISHNU mild
    and calm,
GANESA, SAKRA, ISWARA, the GOD OF KATRAGAM,
The SUN-GOD and the SNAKE-GOD, all high supernal
    Powers,
Bestow a bounteous blessing upon this world of ours !

5

The Prelude to the Legend.

In days of BHUWANEKA, the mighty King, whose sword
Brought victory in all battlefields unto its dauntless
    lord,
Whose head with BUDDHA'S favour was gloriously
    crowned,
Whose ears with gladness ever heard the holy doctrine
    sound !

* See Notes.

6

Beneath that lofty monarch, an Officer of State
Was clothed with mighty power, with honours rich and
    great;
Descended from a race renowned, of high descent and
    far,
Was valiant SEPĀLA, the noble Adigar! *

7

Pure as the enamel of a shell [or pure as is a star],
The Maiden was who grandsire called that noble
    Adigar!
Her beauty like a goddess's did radiantly glow :
And soft and graceful were her words: her voice was
    sweet and low !

8

KING RAJASINHA'S fame* was high as is a royal tower ;
And in his Court, protected by the shadow of his power—
The shadow of his kingly feet, that wealth and joy
    bestowed—
In fortunate tranquillity and happiness abode

9

One whom the world admiringly held high in fame and
    pride,
The Chieftain ATTANAYAKA. The maid became his
    bride.
Unto his godlike stem she clung, as of the golden vine
The tender, trembling tendrils spread, and round the
    branches twine !

       * See Notes.

10

Pure as the badge of sandalwood by high-born damsels
    worn
Upon their brows, she radiant shone; and modestly was
    borne
Her soft and graceful beauty—for beauty sweet and rare
Graced ever MENIKHĀMI, the Lady Jewel fair!

11

Her, with her eyes long [almond-shaped], no being could
    outshine
In all the world's vast, teeming womb, unless he were
    divine!
Towards the precious TRIPLE GEM,* wherein no fault is
    seen,
Her faith was ever perfect, and constant, and serene!

12

Her eggs as guards the plover, as guards the yak his
    tail,
Unceasingly: so never did that pious lady fail
On holy tides the eight great rites* to pay; nor did *one*
    day
See her five duties left undone, ere it had passed away!

13

Her mind, her ear, her wealth, which still in rare pro-
    fusion flowed,
On Buddha, on the Word, and Priests, she plenteously
    bestowed.

* See Notes.

Search all the wide world over, where'er shall one be
    found
To vie in this with her who loved to hear the doctrine
    sound ?

14

The Maker, when the world was shaped, first brought
    to life above,
The nymph that rules o'er Beauty, the nymph that rules
    o'er Love !
And, seeing they were beautiful, no further doubt was
    there,
In perfect loveliness was made the Lady Jewel fair ! *

15

Though all the streams and rivers their floods in ocean
    pour,
The sea, serene and placid, will ne'er o'erleap the shore !
So she, though wealth's broad channels brought to her
    many a prize,
Grew never proud or haughty, but modest, mild, and
    wise :

16

Because her mind was like a gem of purest form and
    light ;
Because her eyes like sapphires shone, with happy
    radiance bright
[Because, in truth, she was as dear as jewels rich and
    rare] ;
The Dame was MENIKHĀMI called, the Lady Jewel
    fair !

* See Notes.

17

If Elu, Páli, Sanskrit books, that fair-eyed Lady read,
Save where the proper pause* should be, her voice was
 never stayed.
Her dark,* dark hair in braided folds like to a cloud
 hung low !
Her arching eyebrows, fair to see, resembled INDRA'S
 bow !

18

And gloriously beautiful her face did shine and glow,
As shines the bright, full Moon in heaven upon the
 earth below!
Her far-extended charity to all the world was shown,
As is a mother's tender love to all her children known !

19

This high-born Lady sought from me, the writer of this
 song,
To sing of legendary lore our Faith has cherished long :
With heart devout and prayerful the sweet request was
 made ;
And thus it was that I with joy this Lay of old essayed.

20

The boundless depth of virtues of the Founder of our
 Faith,
" I with great pride shall sing !" if one heroically saith ;
'Tis as if with mosquito's tooth he should straightway
 endeavour
To pierce Mount Meru's sacred hill* and make its rocks
 dissever !

* See Notes.

21

If in the progress of this Lay which I, the Minstrel,
    sing,
Grave faults occur, set them aside, nor in contention
    bring;
But listen with attentive ears, all men by study wise,
To BUDDHA'S great perfections, whose faith and fame we
    prize ! *

22

The Legend.

There was a town, a stately town, on DAMBADIVA'S *
    shore—
That land which shines resplendent in wealth and
    precious store,
That seems a place where all the wealth of all the world
    is piled !
And on its shore magnificent the city SEWET smiled.

23

With boundaries like those that part Snake-World and
    skyey realm,
That city, which exceeding wealth seemed almost to
    o'erwhelm,
Was girded by a deep sunk moat, that all the walls
    embraced,
And by a rampart strong and high, with gems and
    crystals graced.

24

Upon the lofty turret tops the golden streamers flew,
And danced all merrily whene'er the sportive breezes
    blew ;

* See Notes.

As ever dance on Himalaya's far and snowy hills
The elfin troop from fairyland that know not human
    ills!

25

And when the fair-eyed women danced beside the crys·
    tal wall,
Their figures were reflected, so lissom, fair, and tall,
It seemed as if the goddesses from every point came
    down,
To learn and practise dancing beside that stately town !

26

Upon the crystal rampart walls when red the moonlight
    fell,
The hare that in the moon is seen* was there reflected
    well,
And seemed like BUDDHA in the days when he a hare
    became,
And leaped, unscathed and fearless, into the heart of
    flame !

27

The town gives homes to many a dame, fair as the golden
    vine :
O'er shell-like necks droop clouds of hair ! mouths like
    the lotus shine !
Their pearly teeth from ruby lips gleamed bright to
    look upon !
Their hands were like to wreaths of gold : their bosoms
    like the swan !

* See Notes.

28

Their faces fair white lilies seemed : their eyes as lilies
  blue !
Their soft and smooth and rounded forms like sea-sand
  soft with dew !
And amorous eyes did revel, beholding them with glee,
As revels deep in lotus blooms the restless honey-bee !

29

With ruby lips that blushed as blush the Na-tree's top-
  most buds,
With gait serene and stately, like the monarch of our
  woods,*
The beauty of the damsels that graced the lordly town,
Who worthily may hope to sing, or tell of their renown ?

30

The lotus lake within the walls was like the sisterhood :
There were swans on either's bosom : and like blue
  lilies would
Glance girlish eyes, brown browed like bees : and in the
  twilight cool,
Dark tresses waved like dark-blue weeds that mantle
  o'er the pool !

31

Of elephants with glittering tusks rare store the town
  was nigh,
White as the flight of snowy cranes that cleave the
  upper sky !

* See Notes.

Like lightning gleamed their harness, all plated thick
    with gold !
As clouds of rain or shower drops, their hosts were
    manifold !

32

As round a king throng multitudes of chieftains of the
    land,
As round Mount Meru's sacred hill vast precipices stand,
So thronged the town with chargers and all their gallant
    train,
Like the long sweep of racing waves upon the boundless
    Main !

33

The endless rows of chariots " dashed down each roaring
    street,"
And waked innumerous echoes that never ceased to beat!
And all the massy chariot wheels with golden flags were
    gay,
And drawn by white and prancing mules equipped in
    brave array !

34

In valour like the War-God of Katragama's shrine,
Who quelled the mighty Titans, themselves a race divine,
The city's gallant warriors, victorious in the field,
Had often tamed the foeman and made his legions yield!

35

Within the prosperous city, renowned as if divine,
Graced with the dazzling splendour that fits a royal
    line,

As reigns the great god Sakra, KING KOSOL reigned in
state,
A prince beloved and honoured, beneficent and great!

36

Like to the bright, full moon that shines when shading
clouds are gone,
For royal virtues far renowned, the mighty Monarch
shone!
His graciousness and clemency brought him undying
fame,
And the strong tide of all men's love bore up his glorious
name!

37

Sweet were his speeches ever, his kindness like a gem :
Like waves his generous gifts were, small heed he paid
to them !
Although himself the Ocean, the laws which are the
strand
He never once o'erleapt, or broke his self-imposed command !

38

The radiance of his glory to foreign Courts was known,
And fired them as the kindling flame on logwood faggots
thrown !
His fame like smoke spread far around, as o'er the
shoulders bare
The locks of royal women float when they unbind their
hair !   .

39

Truth, valour, purity of heart, an ever-generous hand,
The virtues of the olden days, as all may understand,

He cherished even as his life, with unsubdued endeavour,
That King renowned whose name and fame from us shall
    perish never !

40

The three prerogatives* that rest the royal Throne before,
The four high schemes of statecraft, the seven graces
    more,
The ten great virtues, the four rules our sacred Faith
    lays down,
He kept, and ruled his people well within that stately
    town !

41

By favour of the gracious King [in whom all honours
    lie],
The wealthy ANEPIDU was graced with titles high :
For lordly wealth renowned was he, of high repute and
    worth ;
The glory of his generous deeds spread over all the
    earth !

42

That noble built, to grace the Faith with a befitting
    home,
A spacious and a lofty pile, a far-seen glittering dome,
Right costly and magnificent and glorious to behold !
To raise its splendid pinnacles went many a lakh of gold !

43

A fair wihára thus uprose—and DEVRAM was its name :
A very Brahma-heaven it seemed, so peerless was its
    fame !

* See Notes.

Rare was its blossomed garniture of fragrant flower and
    tree:
And to the blossoms with their mouths clung many a
    honey-bee!

44

The turrets of the stately pile shone fair with gems and
    gold,
Like to the nine-gemmed, precious crown, right glorious
    to behold,
Which dwellers in the fourfold realms—Gods, Brahmas,
    human folk,
And nágas—gave to BUDDHA, the truths supreme who
    spoke!

45

Four-square it stood, girt round about by crystal shining
    walls,
A massy rampart and a strong, engirdling all the halls,
Like to the fourfold sacred rules of conduct, ever pure,
Which the high Priesthood, still upright, maintains and
    keeps secure!

46

And when the sparkling gems that shone like "twinkling
    points of fire,"
Glittered on peak and pinnacle, on turret top and spire,
Then was the temple as would be the wombèd heaven
    on high,
Were there a hundred thousand suns and moons within
    the sky!

47

Like thunder through the temple aisles the sound of
    preaching rolled:
Upon the sapphired turret tops each banner's golden fold

Flapped in the breeze and quivered like lightning in the
 sky :
The peacocks saw and clamoured as if a storm were
 nigh !

48

Like to the wombèd sky it shone, that temple proud and
 fair,
With many a glowing picture, with painted ceilings rare,
When crowds of the immortals and Brahmas thither
 came
To offer adoration to the All-Seer's name !

49

And when within the temple walls omniscient BUDDHA
 dwelt,
Gods, Brahmas, men, and nâgas in adoration knelt !
The radiance of their jewelled crowns streamed o'er his
 sacred feet,
And bathed them in rare splendour, as fitting was and
 meet !

50

Within the temple gathered the meritorious bands
Of priests endowed with virtues, who held the high
 commands
Enshrined and treasured in their hearts, a field of
 righteousness,
Obedient ever to the rules our institutes profess !

51

Apparelled in their fragrant robes, when each came from
 his cell,
Their garb that priestly Brotherhood became and gar-
 nished well :

They seemed like to a stately row of elephants arrayed
In gemmed and glittering war-gear on which the sun-
    light played !

52

The chamber where the Faith was taught was fair to
    look upon ;
The chambers of the conquering gods in splendour it
    outshone :
For pendant from its carven eaves the pearl-wrought
    network hung,
And precious gems that glittered bright were seen its
    beams among !

53

There, laying all debate aside, they failed not to declaim,
With eloquence serene and sweet, on BUDDHA'S worth
    and fame,
Each after each, in order due, as was the ancient plan,
When he who eldest was in years was foremost speaking
    man !

54

Once on a time, as they were sate within that council
    hall,
To tell the story of a priest who erred, it did befall,
Of one who donned the holy robes, but wearied with the
    rites
And discipline, forsook them soon for sensuous delights !

55

Then BUDDHA, in his chosen place, that still was perfumed
    well
(A habitation excellent, like that where Brahmas dwell),

Where, on the ever-fragrant cloths that draped his
    gorgeous bed,
Serene he sat, and o'er the world delights and blessings
    shed,

56

Heard with his godlike ears that tale the Brotherhood
    disclose
With all exactitude. At once from off the couch he rose,
And on the earth that did, well-pleased, his happy
    advent greet,
He sought in majesty to place his ever-sacred feet.

57

Ere he, the Lord Supreme, who is with every merit
    graced,
His shining feet upon the ground majestically placed,
To bear that ever sacred twain, ere they on earth had
    trod,
A seven-budded lotus burst all blooming from the sod !

58

A double, gold-red robe that draped o'er navel and o'er
    knee,
He wore : and fitting robe it was, and glorious to see !
Rich was the dye, a richer ne'er graced fabric of the
    loom,
Its colour mocked in brilliancy the choicest garden
    bloom !

59

Around this robe his baldric gleamed right beautiful and
    fair,
Delighting every eye that saw, as gleams in upper air

The quivering lightning's vivid flash, with sheen that
    ether fills,
Darting around the golden top of the great King of
    Hills !

60

In colour like the nuga * fruit, an upper robe he wore,
That Lord Supreme, whose name and fame devoutly we
    adore !
His body shone resplendently, as shines the Moon on
    high,
Bathed in the sunset's ruddy glow athwart the purpling
    sky.

61

The radiance of his beauteous form, pre-eminently
    bright,
That yields to gods and mortal men a wonderful de-
    light,
The radiance of the sixfold rays * a matchless lustre
    shed,
In such a rare, resplendent wise as shall below be
    said !

62

Like to the river Jumna [when joyously it flows
From its first home among the hills of everlasting
    snows] ;
Like sapphire or blue lotus, the rays of blue—the dye
Divine and peerless—overspread the firmament on high;

63

Like waters of the Northern Sea, when laughing wavelets
    play ;
Like to Mount Meru's sacred cone, if it should melt
    away,—

         * See Notes.

B

The ever-glorious, golden rays unto the farthest bound
Of the horizon sparkling leapt, and ran and shone
    around ;

64

And far and brilliantly beamed forth the red, red rays
    divine,
Red as the ruby, or the cloud that glows at day's de-
    cline ;
Or like the blushing gleams and glints of shining coral
    seas,
Or blossomed beauty, rosy red, of choicest garden * trees.

65

And pure white radiance too was there, like to the
    herald star,
Day's harbinger ; or like as was in olden times afar
(The Golden Age) the Milky Sea, with billows ever
    white ;
So shone the pure, white Buddha-rays, and bathed the
    worlds in light !

66

Hued like the myrobolan * seed, did other rays divine
Beyond the far horizon's verge with rare resplendence
    shine ;
And made the Brahmans and the gods, who there with
    gifts did stand, .
Gleam like the lapping tongues of flame or blazing fire-
    brand !

67

And other glorious radiance too from every point burst
    forth
[From Eastern bounds to Western, from fronting South
    and North],

        * See Notes.

And seemed like painted cloths adorned with every
    earthly hue,
Held up, unrolled, and spread abroad to the beholder's
    view.

68

That blessed sixfold radiance from BUDDHA'S form that
    sprung,
Streamed far and wide, and low and high, all Nature's
    realms among ;
Descended to the lowest depths, the world of viewless air,
And, mounting, reached the highest realms where beings
    never were.

69

Thus came the great Chief Teacher forth on that
    auspicious day,
From his abode of fragrance rare, where he in grandeur
    lay :
So stalks the royal lion forth, with stately gait and
    brave,
From where the golden rocks conceal his solitary cave !

70

Within the gorgeous Council Hall he took his lordly seat,
With throngs of preachers of the Word assembled at
    his feet;
He was as is the autumn Moon rejoicing on her way
Athwart the sky, attended by the circling stars' array.

71

'Twas thus he spoke, the Lord Supreme, unto the
    Brotherhood
[As they in reverent silence there before his presence
    stood] :—

"Before We came to this, your Hall, what was the
    theme you chose
To hold your high discussions on?   That theme to Us
    disclose."

72

Then from among the Brotherhood, steeped as in nec-
    tared sweet
Of that celestial eloquence, arose, as was most meet,
One of the brethren, high in rank, and kind and sweet
    in mien,
And to the sacred presence stepped, all slowly and
    serene.

73

Prone on the ground he fell; the five meet reverent
    motions * made,
While fervent worship glowed within; then upwards
    o'er his head,
Which was as is a temple shrine, his flower-like hands
    he placed:
'Twas as it were a sacred shrine with fragrant blossoms
    graced.

74

"Great Lord Supreme! who hast destroyed Sin's deadly
    blight and curse,
The thirty-two forbidden themes * thy righteous rules
    rehearse—
Forbidden themes, which never may thy servants speak
    upon;
Of these, this day, obediently, we have not chosen
    one.
                  * See Notes.

75

" We spoke of one who once obeyed thy sacred rules and
laws,
But soon forsook them utterly, vile sensuous lusts the
cause ;
And clinging to those low desires, no longer he observed
The discipline of hermit-life, but from its guidance
swerved.

76

" All weary of our priestly rites, and throwing off control,
He rooted out and killed the faith that glowed within
his soul.
Yet lives he still ; and on the fate that may to him be-
fall,
Have we this day discussion held within our Council
Hall."

77

When thus that ancient Brother had addressed the
gathered crowd,
The Lord Supreme, who listened there, at once replied
aloud
With gracious words :—" The BŪDISAT * himself in days
of yore,
Felt love for women glow and burn within his bosom's
core.

78

" [For, though a king, through that strong love] he
menial service wrought,
And bitter grief and usage hard he bore with patient
thought;

* See Notes.

Till all the wishes of his heart eventually he gained,
And to a lofty height of fame all gloriously attained !"

79

When he had said these gracious words, the ancient
    Brother there
Preferred unto the Lord Supreme his earnest wish and
    prayer
To hear that legend duly told: and thus upon that
    day
Did BUDDHA then rehearse to them what follows in this
    Lay !

END OF THE FIRST PART.

PART II.

The Realm of Malala.

80

In DAMBADIVA'S lordly bounds there lay the noble land
Of MALALA, where perfect weal and joy went hand in
hand :
Within that land the heart found nought that was not
fair and good :
There, KUSĀVATI'S royal town* in stately grandeur stood.

81

Around the crystal rampart-walls a shining moat was
seen,
That rivalled Heaven's broad river in ever-brilliant
sheen ;
It was as was that sacred flood round Kailas' Mount *
that curled,
When SIVA on the high hill-top in mazy dances whirled.

82

The women of that royal town were like the *Wishing
Tree*,*
Their mouths and eyes, its blossomed flowers, right
beautiful to see ;

* See Notes.

Palms, lips, and feet were like the leaves beside the
    tender shoot ;
Their full-orbed bosoms like that tree's ambrosial precious
    fruit.

83

Pure was the northern breeze, that blew from forest far
    away,
Which shook the spray of sandal-trees ; and on the
    youths at play
Refreshingly it breathed and cooled their heated limbs,
    and then
Bestowed on them a fresh desire to try their sports
    again.

84

Save GANESA, or NĀGA-GOD, who should the high re-
    nown
Describe of the fair dames and girls who dwelt within
    the town,
When, beauteous they, as golden vines, in glad and free
    array,
· Went to the garden pleasances all sportively to play ?

85

Upon the upper balconies at ball the maidens played :
Fair as the full-orbed silver Moon was every damsel's
    head ;
Their soft and tender loveliness might fitliest compare
To LAKSHMI'S,* Beauty's goddess fair, the free and de-
    bonair !

* See Notes.

86

Within that royal city were fair parks and pleasances,
Made beautiful surpassingly by rows of stately trees ;
There, choicest fruit and buds and flowers were ever to
be found,
And massy branches that outspread their bourgeoned
limbs around.

87

The pleasances held many a tank and many a spacious
pool,
Well-stored with water, crystal clear, and pure and ever
cool :
Rare sapphires gleamed upon the marge ; and o'er the
tranquil tide,
Hovered the honey-loving bee, and golden swans did
glide.

88

The fleet and gallant racers' hoofs smote earth with
thundering tread,
And swirls of dust uprising there the firmament
o'erspread.
The youngsters from the royal town, fond youth and
laughing boy,
Nought suffering from the sun's hot rage, walked forth
abroad in joy.

89

And many an elephant was there, high-spirited and
strong :
Their tusks upon the right hand side were stout and
huge and long :

With feet, trunk, tail, and massy limbs well-planted on
    the ground,
Full many a noble beast like that within the town was
    found.

90

Like to a throng of lions were the troops of horses
    there,
Of lions [fierce and ravenous, that leave their jungly
    lair]
That with their cruel, branchy claws the skulls have
    split and rent
Of elephants, and all their flanks with gouts of gore
    besprent.

91

And rows of chariots numberless within the city were,
With seats luxuriously equipped, and hangings white
    and fair ;
Right beautiful they were, in sooth, with spiry crests of
    gold,
And golden banners on their tents, that shook as on
    they rolled.

92

And hosts of stalwart warriors, a great and mighty
    band,
Each bearing choicest weapons still within his brawny
    hand ;
And each in armour well equipped of mail from head to
    heel,
Marched ever through the streets and lanes in panoply
    of steel.

93

The deafening din of elephants, of cars, and thronging
  folk,
And champing steeds, throughout the town in all directions broke :
With bursts of music, of five sorts, it mingled ; and the
  sound
Was as if Ocean's foamy surge were roaring all around !

94

The citizens and all the hosts that dwelt the land
  within,
In former births wrought virtuous deeds and cleansed
  their hearts from sin.*
And thus it chanced that o'er the realm, upon a later
  day,
King OKĀVAS, a prince renowned, held firm and
  gracious sway.

95

His fame's bright flower throughout the world shone
  clear, and spread afar,
As in the pond shine lotus flowers, whose stamens like
  a star,
Or multitudinous stars, gleam forth ; whose leaves are
  like a cloud,
And glorious flower-cups as the Moon, serene and fair
  and proud.

96

The Sun, whose fervour varies oft throughout the
  circling year ;
The Moon, that, waning month by month, doth ne'er the
  same appear ;

  * See Notes.

The shaking, breeze-blown Ocean: not these, though great they be,
Could *he* be likened to, for ne'er was king so staunch as he.

97

The lustre of his glory to hostile kings was known :
It pierced their hearts, and, like the blaze of fire, flaming shone.
Then were the royal women's hearts with that great fame possessed ;
Their kindling looks and glowing eyes the fiery truth confessed.

98

His prosperous hand was like unto the firmament on high ;
His sword like RĀHU,* ever strong, who dwells within the sky.
As RĀHU swallows sun and moon, so did *his* glorious fame
Swallow up that of hostile Courts, and put them all to shame.

99

That King, a world-saviour, did in statecraft all excel
[For hard he strove and earnestly to rule his people well].
His train of princely ministers and wise men of the lands,
He summoned to his Council Hall to frame his high commands.

* See Notes.

100

Adorned right gloriously with gems that shone with
    gleamy blaze
[As jewels shine when on their edge the flickering sun-
    light plays],
Young damsels, blooming, blithe, and fair, in shapely
    form and face,
As are the goddesses, were there, endowed with every
    grace.*

101

Of dames and maids of honour graced in such a glorious
    sort,
Full sixteen thousand there abode within the royal
    court:
Chief Queen of the Zenana, the first and fairest there,
Was peerless SĪLAVATI, the exquisitely fair.

102

The Monarch ever graciously—for he was good and kind
Of heart—with parent's tender love his people bore in
    mind;
The several virtues which, observed, best grace the royal
    crown,
With constant care he kept, and ruled within the stately
    town !

103

To guard the land in after-times, nor let it be forlorn,
A prince the people all desired, but none had yet been
    born
Unto her lord by that fair Queen of worth and virtuous
    fame,
And full of those fair charities that deck a royal dame !

* See Notes.

104

To subjects, well or ill disposed, of whatsoever mind,
The ministers were courteous still, benevolent and kind;
All earthly customs well they knew, by lengthened study
    wise
In all the lore and sciences that men of wisdom prize.

105

One day these princely ministers, an ever loyal train,
With all the noble citizens within the king's domain,
Unintermittingly in throngs approached and made resort
Unto the inner citadel, where held the King his court :

106

Then standing by the city gates, the thickly gathered
    crowd,
With voices like as if the sea around were roaring loud,
Cried clamorously : " Is then this town, this royal town
    of thine,
With all its grand and glorious gifts to perish and de-
    cline ? "

107

The King of men the clamour heard, and throwing open
    wide
The windows [of his palace-tower, of massy strength and
    pride],
Looked out straightway upon the crowd of his assembled
    folk ;
And thus with wise and measured words the Monarch
    calmly spoke :—

108

"We wot not, lieges, any faults the practice which debar
Of those fair royal virtues that our privileges are.

Why come ye, then, with clamorous throats, and in our
    presence cry—
The land shall surely perish, Sire !—We ask the reason
    why."

109

When thus the Monarch had addressed the throng of
    listening folk,
The ministers unto the King this answer straightway
    spoke :—
" Hereafter to preserve the world, nor let it be forlorn,
To thee, O Sire, nor prince nor girl has ever yet been
    born.

110

"Wherefore, unto our stately town and all this fair
    domain,
If hostile kings should ever come and o'er us seek to
    reign,
Hereafter will they sorely spoil the land and work it
    woe :
And hence we came to thee, O Sire ! . . . We came and
    clamoured so ! "

111

This speech the Monarch having heard, then made re-
    joinder free :—
" How shall a son be born to us, I pray you tell to me ? "
Thus when the Monarch had addressed the surging
    throng of folk,
The retinue of ministers this answer straightway spoke:—

112

" O Sovereign Lord, illustrious ! the dancing-girls who
    dwell
Within the royal city here we pray thee to expel :

Send them afar in other realms, if so they will, to roam,
Nor let them find beneath thy ward a shelter or a home.

113

" If none of them from out of all their numerous array
Shall bear a child, we pray thee, Sire, to send still more
    away :
We pray thee, Sire, to send away *all* women from the
    town,
Save only her, the chiefest Queen, who shares thy throne
    and crown !

114

" From the blest womb of some of these, to whom rare
    merits cling,
If the fair child we all desire to life and light shall
    spring,
Let us through him preserve the realm, O gracious
    King and Lord ! "
Thus did the sages answer make and speak with one
    accord.

115

The Monarch treasured carefully the saying in his mind :
For love of children swayed him much, and did his
    fancy bind.
And of the dwellers in the town fair damsels not a
    few
He sent outside, and from them all his guardianship
    withdrew.

116

In order to accomplish what the ministers had said,
Of all the sixteen thousand there, to each fair dame and
    maid,

To leave the town straightway the King vouchsafed his
  high consent;
And faring forth, in several ways, beyond the walls they
  went.

117

When all these pains were taken, yet still it did befall,
Of all those fair, departing dames not one among them
  all
An infant bore [so much desired to grace that royal
  home]:
Then did the ministers again and other people come—

118

The citizens within the town—upon a certain day,
And gathered in a mighty throng, unshrinking in array.
Right to the Palace Gate they went, and, near the
  massive door,
They raised again a clamorous cry, as they had done
  before.

119

The King, when he the clamour heard, arose, and thus
  he spoke:
" We have performed what you desired and said, O
  thronging folk !
Beyond the city walls we sent the women far away,
From many a sheltering lodge where they within our
  wardship lay.

120

" And now, since still this circumstance the fates have
  made befall,
That not a child has yet been born by one among them
  all,—

Since nought but this the ruling powers to our deserts
    allow,
What now is fit and meet to do ?   We pray you answer
    now ! ''

121

The Monarch's words were uttered : and then the
    listening crowd
Of citizens who heard his speech thus made reply aloud:
'' Of all the dames and damsels who left our city's bound,
Not one of even small desert, O Sire, was to be found !

122

'' Because of their so small desert, no blessing on them
    rests ;
No infant draws his life from them [or clasps their
    rounded breasts] :
Hence other means must be devised, and other course
    pursued,
That so a prince be born to us to save the multitude.

123

'' But there is one, of pure descent and peerless lineage
    high,
Whose fame is spread through all the lands, o'er all the
    earth and sky :
Her heart is kind and cordial, Sire, and noble and
    serene ;
Majestic in her stateliness is she, thy royal Queen !

124

'' Her teeth are white as are the buds upon the jasmine
    spray ;
Like to the tender leaves her lips ; and little dimples play

The while she smiles all graciously: such is her magic
    grace,
Men's eyes and hearts are captive ta'en by her enchant-
    ing face !

125

"She, SĪLAVATI, thy chief Queen, so glorious and fair,
If from the city's bounds she went, would yield thy
    throne an heir."
Thus did the sages answer make [all gathered in a ring,
When they respectfully stood up and counsel gave the
    King].

126

The King attentively heard all the sages did advance,
And straightway he, so that he might the wide world's
    weal enhance,
Adorned with all the choicest gems, the choicest and
    most rare,
His Queen, the foremost Queen of all, the radiantly
    fair !

127

As if a nymph had left her own celestial home on high,
And, parting from great SAKRA* there, flashed down-
    ward through the sky ;
So, that she might possess a child, then did the royal
    Queen
Leave kingly spouse and court behind, and forth she
    fared serene.

128

Thus when that fair-eyed lady sore affliction's fire
    endured,
The glory of her worth and grace erelong relief pro-
    cured :

---

* Or INDRA the King of the Gods. See note to the fourth stanza.

The King of Gods' cold, rocky throne glowed bright
    with sudden heat,
And red as redhot iron blades, so hot became the seat !

129

As SAKRA with his thousand eyes gazed over every
    land,
The hapless Queen, with heart distraught, he saw dejected
    stand :
His godlike eye revealed to him that to her blessed
    womb
Two radiant gods illustrious from Heaven's high town*
    should come !

130

Then entering first the BŌDISAT'S blest, skyey palace fair,
And next unto another God's, did SAKRA straight re-
    pair :
Benign he said :—" Go to the world of men, that distant
    scene,
And there be born from out the womb of yon delightful
    Queen."

131

The saying of the King of Gods unto their hearts they
    took ;
Then bathed they in his feet's bright rays that shone as
    shines a brook :
"Let us be so conceived," they said, when they the order
    heard,
" *Within the womb of yonder Queen, even as the Lord de-*
    clared ! "

* See Notes.

132

That SAKRA heard, while in his soul sprung up increasing joy ;
Then straightway sought his godlike form to alter and destroy.
A form that to beholders' eyes and minds inspired disgust,
He took, and seemed a feeble man bowed down unto the dust,

133

With eyes all bleared and full of tears, with wrinkled cheeks and wan,
With mouth from which the teeth had dropt—in sooth, an ancient man !
Like to a Brahman very old, with want and sorrow bowed,
The mighty SAKRA seemed, and thus approached the thronging crowd.

134

Then shivering like a scarecrow vile, that in the fields is tied,
Did SAKRA come in Brahman guise. To him the crowd applied ;
And many folks assembled round with tricky wiles did say :—
"[Father of rags innumerable !] what brings you here to-day ? "

135

Now in the midst of that great throng was many a noble head,
Forthwith in front of whom he went : then, with a god-like tread

And majesty, the King of Gods beside the Queen stept
　　straight,
And took her hand and led her forth beyond the city
　　gate.

136

Unto a wretched little cot, the feeblest e'er designed,
With boltless door, without a wall to shield it from the
　.　wind,
That had of goods for household use not e'en the slightest
　　store,
He took the stately Queen, and said: "Here did we dwell
　　of yore !

137

" To all the places round I go, and rice and betel seek :
Until I come, pray rest you here." Thus did the ancient
　　speak.
Then on a rough, unshapely couch he made the lady rest
And sleep, and with soft, loving hands her body rubbed
　　and pressed.

138

Thereafter then right speedily he bore to Heaven's high
　　town
The Queen, and used that power of flight that only Gods
　　may own
All gloriously : and then on couch divine, with hangings
　　rare,
Within a golden palace meet, lay tranced the lady fair.

139

A week the queenly dame lay there asleep, and then she
　　rose
From off the couch, and stood erect right in the midst of
　　those

Full two-and-thirty deities. Then SAKRA to their view
Appeared, and at his feet she bowed with lowly reverence
   due.
                                   .

140

The rays that from his eye dart down did rest upon her
   face
As on the seven-budded blooms the clustering bees find
   place.
He said : " A gracious boon and meet on you shall I bestow :
If you accept it, evermore will blessings from it flow."

141

He spoke, and joyfully the Queen at once made answer
   free :
" A glorious boy ! if thou but grant that jewel unto me,
Great boon and precious will it be ! " He heard the words
   she said,
And straightway thus unto her prayer the God rejoinder
   made :

142

" Two sons on thee shall I bestow [to glad thy heart and
   eyes] :
Of these shall one ill-favoured be, yet upright still and
   wise :
Right beautiful, and yet a fool, shall be the other one.
Now, which of these dost thou prefer to be thy first-born
   son ? "

143

The words by SAKRA uttered she heard, and straight
   replied :
" What better is than wisdom, Sire, in all the world beside?

Then let the child with wisdom graced be first-born son
    to me,
And him that is but beautiful, O let him second be !"

144

Then SAKRA gave unto the Queen, and filled her heart
    with glee,
Sweet kusa grass, and godlike robes, the heart of sandal-
    tree
With scent divine, a soft guitar of rare melodious power,
And from the tree that grows in Heaven a sweetly
    blossomed flower.

145

He took the dame, and to the earth all gloriously hied,
And placed her on a goodly couch her royal spouse be-
    side.
He touched the navel with his foot : and mighty SAKRA
    then,
" *Be fruitful !*" said, and straightway winged to Heaven
    his flight again !

END OF THE SECOND PART.

PART III.

King Kusa's Birth and Upbringing: The Search for his Bride.

146

Possessed of attributes that may such stage of life befit,
An undeveloped BUDDHA yet, our BŌDISAT ['tis writ]
Did thus from Heaven's high citadel majestically come,
And enter straightway at that time Queen SĪLAVATI'S
    womb.

147

The King, that instant waking, then gazed with eyes of
    love
And great affection on the Queen the royal couch above;
Then he besought her to declare each circumstance and
    all
To him as unto her did each and all of them befall.

148

From the first hour when forth the Queen went from her
    royal home,
[That childless she might be no more, but back rejoicing
    come],

Until the hour when she returned, what did to her befall,
Then did the Queen recount to him, each circumstance
and all.

149

The kusa grass and other gifts the King of Gods be-
stowed
Upon herself, the stately Queen majestically showed;
And how it was declared that she should childless be no
more,
That lady to her royal spouse the tale recounted o'er.

150

The Monarch heard all joyously, and summoned every
priest
And Brahman there at once to hold high festival and
feast.
Not few the precious alms he gave : and then, with proud
array
Of great processions, forth he went in honour of the day.

151

The radiance of her beauty shone all queenly, fair, and free,
As shines the Moon's pale shower of beams upon the
Milky Sea :
Like which was still her husband's love. And then, as
days flew by,
She felt the longings women feel before their time comes
nigh.

152

A paleness rare and soft and pure suffused her every
limb;
From day to day her dainty waist waxed evermore less
slim;

There spread around her nippled breasts a purple-bluish
 rim;
The radiance of her eyes and face grew day by day more
 dim.

153

Now when the months in number due their course had
 fully run,
That queenly dame right beautiful gave birth unto a son.
Ill-favoured was his countenance, devoid of beauty's
 trace;
Yet still his worth and merits high bestowed upon him
 grace.

154

Prince KUSA was the name bestowed upon that royal
 prince,
High and auspicious, who right soon rare merit did
 evince:
The love that parents feel for sons, the warmest, fondest
 love,
On him abundantly was shed, and thus he grew and
 throve.

155

Now, when the darling little child, the wisdom-gifted
 one,
Began to lift his tiny foot and learn to walk alone,
Another God from Heaven's high town [flashed down
 the sky serene,
And] was conceived within the womb of that delightful
 Queen.

156

As from the bosom of dense clouds the stately Moon
 walks forth
In might and majesty divine, and beams on nether earth,

So from his mother's womb appeared, all radiantly bright,
Another darling prince beloved, and saw this world's fair
    light.

157

That prince was very beautiful, and to him they assigned
The name of JAYANPATI, with joyous heart and mind:
Nor tender love was wanting there, but amply shed
    upon
Him as he grew, was the fond love that parents bear a
    son.

158

Like to the Sun and Moon in heaven [which men still
    love to view],
With all that did befit their rank, the royal brothers
    grew:
And when Prince KUSA had attained unto his sixteenth
    year,
E'en as the Eye of all Three Worlds did that young
    Prince appear.

159

The kingly father took delight and never-ceasing joy
In the fair progress and pursuits of his right royal boy,
Who gazed with eyes of wisdom keen upon the further
    shore
Of Arts and Sciences' great sea, and crossed its waters
    o'er.

160

[Now did the King] call unto him, upon a certain tide,
The Queen, with rarest beauty graced, and took her
    straight aside:
And then addressing unto her full many a tender word,
Sweet words [that ladies love to hear], he thus with her
    conferred :—

161

" For that loved son of yours, dear wife, for worth so
    far renowned,
High time it is, it seems to me, a bride should now be
    found—
The daughter of a royal sire, one graced with beauty
    rare,
And, as the goddesses above, all radiantly fair !

162

" Then, to your son pray go at once; and to that princely
    boy
[So that he may right royal bliss and happiness enjoy]
Convey this message straight, nor let the matter be de-
    layed :
And then return to me ! " the King with joyous accents
    said.

163

As if the words new life infused, the joyful Queen gave
    ear,
And called a maiden to her side, one who stood ever near—
One who, whene'er occasion called, in fitting phrase could
    speak,
Accomplished, graceful, willing too, a gentlewoman meek,

164

A damsel winning in her ways. She told her what her
    lord
Had said, minutely point by point, each several phrase
    and word ;
Then, sending her unto the Prince, she bade her straight
    unfold
To him exactly and at length what has above been told.

165

The damsel went and saw the Prince, and knelt upon
    her knee,
And reverence paid unto his feet that glorious were to
    see :
Then, rising, stood she at one side, and, leaving nothing
    hid,
Him every word and all she told, e'en as she had been
    bid.

166

The speech he heard :—" Why speak of this? why speak
    of this to me ?
A hideous face like this of mine no bride could gladly
    see,
Or love, or love to live with me.   [I to my fate resign
Myself at once.]   Domestic life can ne'er, I know, be
    mine !

167

" While my good parents live on earth," the Prince beloved
    cried,
" Here [as my presence comforts them] shall I with joy
    abide :
Thereafter, when the time shall come, within a hermi-
    tage
A hermit's life, high-prized on earth, shall crown my
    latter age ! "

168

He spoke : [in sooth, a bitter speech for one high-born
    and young],
And all the words [that so had flowed from his mellifluous
    tongue]

The damsel hastened to the Queen without delay to
    bring :
And straight the Queen informed her lord, the sorely
    grieving King.

169

Yet thus, thereafter from that day, Prince KUSA often
    thought :—
" If what my royal father wills be executed nought
By me, it will be ominous and sore and grievous thing ;
For I am bound to do the work appointed by the King."

170

Then once again he thought :—" My fault, my fault will
    I to-day
By stratagem and shrewd device completely do away,
And glad my parents while they live ; then, in my
    latter age,
Will I retire, as I desire, unto my hermitage ! "

171

Straightway he sent unto the one Chief Goldsmith of
    the town,
Of all his craft throughout the world who had the most
    renown,
A rare and cunning workman he (so is the story told)
[And deftly skilled to plan and shape whate'er is made
    of gold].

172

" This mass of gold I give to you " (thus did the Prince
    command)
" Mould in the shape of goddess fair, one of the heavenly
    band.

When all is done, come back to me, nor long returu
delay!"
Thus to the Craftsman spoke the Prince, and sent him
straight away.

173

That very day the BŌDISAT, by virtue of his skill
[A power which moulded everything unto his potent
will],
Wrought out of thick and massy gold a shape divinely
fair,
Surpassing even goddesses in choicest beauty rare :

174

Her limbs he robed in drapery, ethereal, flowing fair ;
Round neck and arms rare gauds he placed with tasteful
art and care.
That golden image, so devised by his all-skilful hand,
In a bedchamber glorious he straightway caused to
stand.

175

Now, on the day the Goldsmith came with joyful heart
and will,
And showed the golden figure he had shaped with
curious skill :
Right beautiful it was in truth, for great was his
renown ;
And carefully he brought it forth and blithely set it
down.

176

Now, when the Lordly One had seen that figure passing
fair :
"Go to the chamber glorious, and, looking round it
there,

A golden statue wrought by me within it will you
  find :
Go, bring it forth and set it here," he said with tranquil
  mind.

177

Then went the Master Goldsmith forth, and saw the
  statue there,
The golden figure glorious, that shone surpassing fair :
He thought a goddess had come down from heaven to
  nether earth,
By virtue of the Lordly One's all-sovereign power and
  worth.

178

When he came back, he straightway spoke unto the
  Lordly One :—
" Thy queenly bride all gloriously within the chamber
  shone,
Bright as the Moon ! As all alone she stood within
  the room,
I did not dare to venture in : so back to thee I come."

179

Thus having said, the Craftsman made, as low he louted
  down,
Meet reverence to the feet of him, that Prince of high
  renown.
Then said the Prince :—" No bride is there, O man in
  metal great !
'Tis but a statue wrought of gold : go, bring it hither
  straight."

D

180

He spoke : and straightway forth was brought the golden
    image fair,
Attired in rich and costly robes, such robes as monarchs
    wear ;
With precious ornaments adorned then was it decked
    and graced,
And on a sumptuous carriage next Prince KUSA had
    it placed.

181

Then said he :—" If a royal dame, the daughter of a king,
With loveliness to equal this, you unto me shall bring,
Then will I choose her for my bride : such is my high
    intent ! " .
Then to his queenly mother he the golden statue sent.

182

That shining figure wrought of gold they showed unto
    the Queen :
It shone as if a nymph from heaven had downward
    flashed serene !
Erect they showed it to the Queen, and told her, one by
    one,
Each several phrase and utterance of her right royal
    son.

183

The Queen, when she the tidings heard, convened with-
    out delay
A council of the ministers.   Amidst their high array,
With sweet and winning speech, and words with nectar-
    essence fraught,
Thus did the royal dame declare her inmost wish and
    thought :

184

" The virtue-gifted Prince of ours has won no small
    renown :
Great SAKRA'S gift, his name and fame through all the
    lands have flown.
Wherefore, O lieges, it is meet a bride of beauty rare,
That may with this fair shape of gold in majesty com-
    pare,

185

" Yea, beautiful exceedingly, the daughter of a King,
Of pure descent, to match my son, you seek and hither
    bring,
That 'neath the canopy of kings, illustriously bright,
They may the royal throne maintain and yield the realm
    delight !

186

" So search the nations round about in order to discover
A royal damsel fair and meet for this right royal lover,
Our noble son, whose rare desert is of such high degree,
That to preserve the whole wide world a worthy one
    were he !

187

" This beauteous golden statue, then, straight bear with
    you away ;
And when the clustering people crowd about the close
    of day,
In places where they gather thick, there set it, and aside
Unseen remain, and keenly watch whatever may betide.

188

" Now, if in any town there be a damsel passing fair,
Delightful to the heart, and one who may with this
    compare ;

And men say—*Such one's daughter is like to this golden shape!*
Hearken unto the pleasant words, and let them not escape.

189

" Thence go, all radiant with joy, the damsel to behold,
And on her, as a gift, bestow this statue fair of gold ;
As to the bridal, ascertain and straight determine all :
Then straight with blithesome hearts return to this our palace hall."

190

Thus making them acquainted with each part of her intent,
She laid her high command on those who forth departing went.
The beauteous figure wrought of gold she trusted to their charge,
And from the city sent them forth to roam the realms at large.

191

The ministers heard every word the gracious Queen had said :
Upon a golden palanquin the image fair they laid,
The image wrought of gold, attired and decked with jewels gay,
And speedily from town to town they hastened on their way.

192

By many a bubbling fountain, by ferry, and by ford,
Where crowds of people thronging come and gather in accord,

The golden statue they set up, and straight aside with-
    drew,
Concealing, while they stood apart, their little group
    from view.

193

From places where the people cried aloud with one
    acclaim,
When they the golden figure saw—*Except a goddess came*
From heaven, there were no form on earth with that one to
    compare !
From all such places forth again the royal train did fare.

194

At last, in MADURATA'S land to SĀGALA they came,
Abounding in all goodly things, a town of wide-spread
    fame ;
In men, steeds, elephants, and cars, it had no small re-
    nown :
It was as if Heaven's citadel had unto earth come down !

195

Unto the king of that fair realm eight daughters had
    been born,
Pure, fair, illustrious [radiant as is a summer morn] !
The eldest, PRABAVATI, immaculate and fair,
The hearts of all men took in thrall, endowed with beauty
    rare !

196

Like as from out the fathomless, immeasurable Main,
A single drop to show the folk, a tiny drop were ta'en,
So, sages, of her loveliness I sing ! drink in the strain
With both your ears, as if you would celestial nectar
    drain !

197

Like to the peacock's feathery train, blue, lustrously out-
    spread,
Her locks shone forth, while blossomed wreaths adorned
    her lovely head,
Like to a cloud, dense, steely-blue, when thick the light-
    nings play
Right vividly !   Such was the dame who held all hearts
    in sway !

198

With beauties rare and manifold that radiant lady
    shone !
If e'er a tiny ringlet curled her narrow brow upon,
And any spot were there, it seemed as seems the Moon
    on high,
When partly hidden by a cloud, a light cloud floating by !

199

Her lovely eyebrows and her nose did likeness meetly
    hold
To banners thick and darkly blue, bound to a staff of
    gold !
To fresh, young gold-banana trees, with long leaves
    darkly blue,
Those lovely features ever bore a marked resemblance
    true !

200

The eyes of that fair damsel, too, the fairest of the earth,
Were deeply, darkly, gleamy blue, provoking joy and
    mirth.
Like sapphires and blue lotus, their hue : their sportive
    gleam
As sparkling sport of fish that dart and play within the
    stream !

201

Like as the lotus bloom allures the bees, a thronging
swarm,
So did that joyous lady's face the eyes of all men charm !
Her lustrous lips disparted were like leaflets fresh and
fair ;
Her shining teeth like filaments of fragrance choice and
rare !

202

Oft her delightful, blooming cheeks were thrown fleet
shadows o'er
By her gold ear-rings twain, wheel-shaped : they seemed
as they were four,
And glittered gaily like the wheels, the four gold wheels
that move
The car of KĀMA, the divine, the sovereign God of
Love ! *

203

Eclipsing three-eyed SIVA's wife,* shone bright that
maiden fair ;
That in the three worlds' ample bounds none might with
her compare,
Her lovely neck glowed ever bright—[a pure and
beauteous place]—
For there it was great BRAHMA set the three rare marks
of grace !

204

Her shapely arms were like the wreaths of champak
flowers * that grace,
In perfect bloom, great KĀMA's head, and deck that
lustrous place !

* See Notes.

Resplendent were those glorious arms as lightning flame
    on high,
Should it in never-ending chain gleam ceaseless o'er the
    sky!

205

Like rounded brows of elephants, of elephants of might,
Were her high swelling, matchless breasts, incomparably
    bright!
The golden cord, with jewels strung, around them, made
    them shine
Like the anointing cups of gold of KĀMA the divine!

206

That royal lady radiant shone as if a goddess high,
All beautiful, to visit earth had left the upper sky!
Her form* was like a golden frame: [Such was her magic
    grace],
The hearts of all men were entranced when they beheld
    her face!

207

Like to a stately tree, the shape of that delightful
    maid:
To climb unto the top if e'er the God of Love essayed,
As cords to help was each fair tress that did her body
    deck,
And the three marks, great BRAHMA set, of beauty on
    her neck!

208

Of a courageous elephant the round, projecting brow
Resembled her deep bosom, where two swelling breasts
    did glow.

* See Notes.

Her dainty waist was slim, as if because the weight it bore
Of her full bosom—slim as shaft of KĀMA's bow of yore!

209

The eyes of men did on her crowd as fish in youth's
  bright stream
(The stream of shining banks), when forth they gaily
  throng and gleam ;
Her rounded, softly-moulded form beamed radiant to behold,
As bright, resplendent chariot-wheels made out of massy
  gold !

210

Her limbs outshone the taper trunk and gold-banana
  stem—
The limbs of that rare damsel how shall I liken them?
Like golden posts they were, to which hot elephants are
  brought
And bound; and bachelors were the fond objects
  caught!

211

And what shall match the lovely knees [all statuesque
  and rare]
Of that sweet dame, who shone as shines a nymph divinely
  fair?
Like one of bubbles twain that spring from forth the
  Northern Sea
Afar, and perish nevermore ; so was each lovely knee !

212

Of that delightful, queenly maid, so radiantly fair,
The smooth, soft, shining lower limbs in lustre might
  compare

With golden peacocks' shining necks, that ever glow and
    thrill !
They did beholders' eyes and hearts with ardent passion
    fill !

213

Beneath her gracious, flower-like feet that rosy red did
    bloom,
Did many swan-like, queenly dames, sweet shelter seek-
    ing, come :
Like blossoms red their fingers shone, bedecked with
    sapphires rare,
And other jewels that might well with clustering bees
    compare.

214

Save SAKRA, or ANANTAYA, who fitting praise could
    sing,
Or mark, the charms of that fair dame, the daughter of
    the King ?
Whose deep full-breasted bosom shone like the projecting
    brow
Of elephants—whose rosy lips like tender buds did
    glow !

215

Now, when the ministers who forth the golden statue
    bore
Reached that fair town [of SĀGALA], they halted by the
    shore,
The shore that girt the royal pond [beside the palace
    gate].
There set they up the shape, and there aside resolved
    to wait.

216

And when the sun had risen, but shortly after dawn,
There came eight damsels [tripping across the myrtled
    lawn] ;
With gold and silver pitchers all joyously they came,
To bathe fair PRABAVATI, the peerless royal dame.

217

And in the midst of that gay throng, that happy girlish
    train,
There walked an aged dame that morn across the fair
    domain,
An aged dame, and crooked too, the foster-mother she
Of radiant PRABAVATI—a post of high degree !

218

That aged dame, when she beheld the golden statue fair,
Supposed it PRABAVATI, and said, with angry air :—
" Alone, alone, O princess ! why hither have you come ?
[What tempted you without your train beside the pool
    to roam ?] "

219

Then vigorously upraising her withered hand beside,
With many a harsh, unwonted word, the scolding matron
    cried :—
" O is it right you cause my death, and work me utter
    woe ? "
Thus did she speak, and on the cheek she dealt a hearty
    blow !

220

Thus, since the things that had occurred before she did
    not know,
Upon the golden statue's cheek she dealt a hearty blow

And, as her hand received a hurt—one neither slight
    nor slow—
Thus spoke the ancient matron then, whom crookedness
    bent low :

221

" Believing it my daughter, I struck with hasty hand
This beauteous statue wrought of gold that doth before
    us stand :
And sore, right sore my hand is hurt ! Forsooth, I well
    may say,
To me a grievous thing has chanced, to me upon this
    day ! "

222

Now, when the words were spoken, forth descended to
    the light
The ministers from where, aside, they hid them out of
    sight.
Their hearts with joy were brimming o'er, with happiness
    full fraught :
And all the truth to ascertain with eagerness they
    sought.

223

" And is there, then, a royal maid, endowed with beauty
    rare,
Who may with this fair shape of gold in loveliness
    compare ?
The truth, the whole truth, tell to us, if this be so, we
    say ! "
Thus did the royal ministers with eager accents
    pray.

224

The speech which they had uttered, the ancient lady
heard,
And answering straight with many a sweet and many a
potent word,
The doubts that nestled in their hearts she made afar
to go :
And thus she spoke, that aged dame, whom crookedness
bent low :

225

" In MADURATA'S lordly realm, in this fair town of ours
Of SĀGALA, there reigns a king of high, puissant powers,
King MADU, ever great and good, whose peerless
daughter fair
Is Princess PRABAVATI named, a dame of beauty rare !

226

" If she into a closet dim, a closet dark and small,
Right in the middle of the house, shall enter, straightway
all
The crowd of gloom, thick gathered there, will be dis-
persed and fly
Afar, as if some jewelled lamps were there hung up on
high !

227

" The fragrance of her beauteous form [all radiant, fresh,
and fair],
Is that of both sweet sandal-woods, an odour choice and
rare !
The sweet, sweet breath of her dear mouth, a very womb
of sweets,
Is that which springs from lotus blooms [and early
morning greets] !

228

"Although, where that fair dame abides, may other
　　maidens be,
Princesses fair of beauty rare, yet none so fair as she !
By her they seem as lamps appear when, lighted every
　　one,
Their blaze declines as on them shines the splendour of
　　the sun !

229

"Now, if you take this shape of gold, right smooth and
　　truly fair,
And place beside that queenly maid, endowed with
　　beauty rare,
So will it seem by her, as would a female wandarú*
By one of the fair nymphs above [who flies bright ether
　　through] !

230

"As beams the autumn Moon in heaven—[of heaven the
　　very Queen] !
With retinue of glittering stars, majestic and serene,
So royal PRABAVATI shines, majestically gay,
As forth she goes in midst of those who form her bright
　　array !"

231

When thus of PRABAVATI'S charm the glowing tale was
　　told
Unto the royal ministers [who brought the shape of
　　gold],
Joy fell increasing on their hearts, upon the hearts of all,
As on the Milky Ocean's waves the placid moonbeams
　　fall !

* See Notes.

232

Then taking up the statue smooth, the statue wrought of
gold,
And entering the palace hall, their message straight they
told
Unto the high Prime Minister, that he might all declare,
The object of their coming forth unto the Monarch
there.

233

Then went the high Prime Minister, and, with profound
salaams,
He on his lofty crown upraised his closely-pressed
palms—
The salutation meet for kings: then straightway he
declared
Unto the King, and point by point, the message he had
heard.

234

The King, the tidings having heard, straight called unto
him then
The ministers, who thither went, eight honourable men :
Greeting and fair encouragement on them bestowed the
King,
As in his royal presence they were gathered in a ring.

235

As to the welfare of the King, the sovereign of the earth
[King OKĀVAS], the Monarch sought; then what had
brought them forth;
Each several circumstance he sought from the assembly
there,
The wealthy ministers who came, and bade them straight
declare.

236

" Full many a thousand miles away on DAMBADIVA'S plain,

King OKĀVAS puissantly protects a fair domain :

Chief King and Emperor is he ; and unto him was given

A gift of SAKRA, the divine, the gracious Lord of Heaven.

237

" That gift is famed Prince KUSA, one well versed in human lore,

Who has on Wisdom's stately ship attained the farther shore

Of Science's great ocean ! Bold as a lion, too,

Is he ! His name and fame are known all nations through.

238

" For him, that Prince most excellent, on us was laid command

To take thy daughter as his bride [the glory of this land] !

And, therefore, hither now we come, conveying it with care,

To offer to her as a gift, this golden statue fair."

239

The Monarch heard the uttered speech, and at the welcome word,

His heart was filled with sovereign joy as if on him were poured

The royal unction once again. Then he, that very day,

Held high and joyous festival in glorious array.

240

On them who thither had conveyed the shape of gold
with care,
An offering to the royal maid, the Princess blithe and
fair—
On them, the King did graciously rare honour straight
bestow—
Upon his guests, the ministers, who bound them forth to
go

241

To DAMBADIVA'S shore again; but ere the realm they
leave,
Rare gifts and precious treasures, too, as presents they
receive,
To bear to sovereign OKĀVAS, from that great King of
might,
Who sent them forth with loving heart, and filled with
rare delight.

END OF THE THIRD PART.

E

PART IV.

───◇───

Ʈhe Bridal of Kusa and Prabavati.

242

Now did the ministers with joy proceed upon their way,
Full many a hundred long, long miles, without or stop
    or stay,
Or one mishap, until at length, their happy journey
    done,
They reached fair KUSĀVATI'S town ; and blithe was
    every one.

243

High salutations and profound, with loyalty and love,
They made to sovereign OKĀVAS [who ruled that realm
    above],
And unto her, his stately Queen : and what to them
    befel
In going forth and coming home, all straightway did
    they tell.

244

The Monarch heard the pleasant words, the welcome
    words they said,
With joyous heart and soul, and straight great prepara-
    tions made,

And marshalled throngs of vassals, that forth they might
    with pride,
Go to the Wedding Festival, and bring the bonny Bride.

245

With fivefold sorts of music, that raised a clangorous cry,
With banners and umbrellas * uplifted to the sky,
The King and his chief Consort, in festival array,
Set forth, and speedily passed o'er the intervening way.

246

As when, a kalpa* ending, the rapid winds commotion
Tempestuous make, and strike and heave on earth the
    mighty ocean ;
Such was the stir when that great host, the gallant, royal
    train,
Swept through the streets of SĀGALA, and éntered its
    domain.

247

His infantry and horsemen, his elephants and cars,
King MĀDU straight assembled [——an army meet for
    wars]
And went to meet his royal guests, and, full of love and
    pride,
[Gave greeting to King OKĀVAS], and called him to his
    side.

248

The Palace next they entered ; and, on the jewelled seat,
Bedecked with snowy drapery, King MĀDU, as was meet,
Then caused his guests to rest themselves: and welcome
    fit and fair
Gone through, it chanced, when both the Kings together
    dwelling were,

* See Notes.

249

That stately SĪLAVATI said, that ever gladsome Queen,
How many a day within the walls already they had
  been,
And told her lord her earnest wish that she, without
  delay,
Might Princess PRABAVATI see, the maiden fair and gay.

250

King MADU of that speech and wish was straightway
  made aware,
And thereupon sent messages to PRABAVATI fair,
How to her husband's kingly sire and mother she should
  go,
And let those royal kinsfolk twain their chosen daughter
  know.

251

A golden vine that climbs aloft the spreading *Wishing
  Tree;*
A golden swan 'midst snowy swans, right beautiful to
  see;
The bright, full Moon, ringed round about by glorious
  orbs of light;
A stately elephant with train of elephants of might :

252

Such, such was PRABAVATI, when forth she came to
  view,
Surrounded by her maidens and foster-mother true,—
That day when she, delightful, and duteous, and serene,
Came forth to greet her parents, the foreign King and
  Queen.

253

As her right royal parents beheld her beauty rare—
Not little was that beauty, for she was passing fair !—
With their own eyes beholding, their hearts with joy were
    fraught,
Joy in abundant measure ; but *this* was what they
    thought :—

254

" If this all-radiant Princess our son shall ever see,
Of visage so ill-favoured, small prospect would there be
Of her abiding with him ; and now what shall we do ? "
Thus meditating, often their minds the thought renew.

255

Keen-witted SĪLAVATI, the rarely-gifted Queen,
Asked—" Let us shape a project, a potent one and
    keen ; "
And thus that royal Lady announced her shrewd design,
Declaring it a custom of her ancestral line :—

256

" From that far-distant period when first, in days of
    yore,
Our kingly line was founded, since then and ever more,
Whene'er to prince a princess, both equal in degree,
Is matched and forth conducted his stately spouse to be ;

257

" Until that bride right royal, and gentle-souled and
    sweet,
Shall feel another life than hers beneath her bosom beat,
Till then, that high-born lady shall ne'er by daylight see
The prince, her royal husband, wherever they may be :

258

"But in the night-tide only will he be by her side:
Nor meet at other seasons the husband and the bride ;
At early morn arising, they part before the dawn :
Such is our line's old custom from distant ages drawn.*

259

" Now fain would I discover if PRABAVATI dear
Hereafter to this usage is willing to adhere :
Ask, therefore, and inform us straight, if such be her
      intent : "
Thus spoke the Queen—and message thus unto King
      MADU sent.

260

The King the message hearing, unto his daughter
      dear
Revealed it all, and insomuch as she made answer
      clear—
"'Tis well ! 'tis well ! so shall it be ! " at once, delaying
      nought,
He to the royal parents twain the daughter's answer
      brought.

261

From these ambrosial words of hers abiding joy did
      spring
Unto the twain, who showered regard and love upon the
      King,
King MADU ; and kind pleasing words, immeasurably
      sweet,
They poured [into his royal ears—a farewell fit and
      meet].

* See Notes.

262

Then, taking PRABAVATI forth, and massed in due
array,
In grand procession on they went, and all the lengthened
way
With speed they passed, until at last they blithely lighted
down
Within the walls and castle-halls of KUSĀVATI'S town.

263

[To grace the day] imprisoned men were from their
bonds set free ;
Birds, in their cages thralled no more, flew chirruping
with glee ;
Tether or yoke no longer held four-footed beasts that
day
[But all in freedom forth might roam, or rest, or idly
play].

264

Rich gold and silver pitchers, graced with blossoms fair
and free
Of cocoa-nuts, abounded there, right beautiful to see !
Parched grain like flowers, and four more flowers, profuse
were scattered wide,
And arches,* decked with gold and gems, arose on either
side.

265

The noble city was adorned as brilliantly that day
As is a city of the gods celestially gay ;
The fivefold sorts of music clanged their far-resounding
cry,
As swept along the gazing throng, the brave procession by.

* See Notes.

266

Then when the feast was over, and bridal rites were
   done,
To KUSA of the noble heart, the gifted, princely one,
The King, the ministers, and folk intrusted, on that
   day,
Their city's welfare and their own, and gave him royal
   sway.

END OF THE FOURTH PART.

PART V.

Queen Prababati's Discobery.

267

As the Queen-Mother had enjoined, ne'er did the Prince
    so dear
By daylight to his queenly Bride at any time appear ;
Yet joyed he in her beauty rare, as, in the realms above,
In RATI, his celestial spouse, did KĀMA, God of Love.

268

The bright effulgence that shone forth from PRABAVATI's
    face
[In loveliness transcending all, a miracle of grace],
Yet to her husband's glory was still as might be seen
The firefly's radiance to the sun's when forth he beams
    serene !

269

Then did that pleasant Sovereign, King KUSA, take de-
    light
In minstrels and in dancers and singers, as was right :
For great was his magnificence, prosperity, and pride.
Ere many days were over, he went and stood beside

270

His mother, the Queen-Mother, and noble greeting
gave ;
And duly first as to her health the royal son did crave :
Then told his wish, his earnest wish, with ardour and
with pride,
To see by day the Princess, his darling and his bride.

271

His words she heard, and straight to him the stately
Queen replied :
" Until another life than hers thy Darling and thy
Bride
Feels beat beneath her bosom, hope not, hope not to
see
By day, the queenly Princess : till then it must not
be ! "

272

Yet, though the high Queen-Mother thus unto her son
had said,
The wish to see the Princess on him incessant preyed
Unchangingly and ceaseless ; and, since it thus befel,
Again the Mother spoke to him, and these fair words did
tell :

273

" Go, hide your royal visage now, quick, cover it with
care,
And where the elephant-keepers stand, straight in the
midst repair :
And as among the grooms you stand, then thither will I
come,
And bring fair PRABAVATI forth, the Bride of rarest
bloom."

274

Then with her radiant daughter, the Queen with joy
went down
Unto the royal stables, and—beasts of high renown—
The great procession-elephants [on which, on festal day,
The King is borne] with joy they saw, and turned to go
away.

275

With pleasure of the rarest sort, King KUSA saw his
Bride,
As thus within the stable stalls he stood the grooms be-
side.
Some dirt lay there upon the floor, he stooped and
gathered it,
And throwing it with violence, the Princess' back he
hit.

276

That lady so assaulted sore, no sooner felt the blow,
Than round she turned, while in her face right royal
wrath did glow :
" Wretch ! to my royal husband shall I, this very day,
Straight shall I speak, that he may wreak the punish-
ment he may ! "

277

She spoke ; and SĪLAVATI then, the proud and royal
dame,
As if with indignation fired, to the offender came,
And harsh and hot and wrathful words she poured upon
his head,
And passionate abuse withal that queenly Lady shed.

278

[Then to her daughter :—] " These rude grooms, the
　　elephants who guard,
Unlawful deeds do ever ; * and [though to bear is hard]
Yet 'tis a good and gracious thing their clownishness to
　　bear,
Nor of their rude, ill-mannered pranks to have a further
　　care."

279

Thus did she speak, and thus consoled her daughter
　　sweet and fair :
And joy increasing in their hearts—a joy benign and
　　rare—
Mother and daughter straight went back to where they
　　dwelt in state,
The high and royal Palace Tower, and entered through
　　its gate.

280

Again, as on the former time, the stately King beside
His Mother stood, and said to her [whatever might be-
　　tide,
Or weal or woe might chance, he said, with eagerness
　　and pride],
How earnest was his wish to see his darling and his
　　Bride !

281

His Mother heard, and straightway said :—" The dress
　　at once assume
Of one who tends our royal steeds ; go garb you as a
　　groom :

* See Notes.

Then in the royal stables stand, and thither I will
    come,
And PRABAVATI call with me, the Bride of peerless
    bloom."

282

Then, where the royal steeds were stalled, forth went
    the queenly dames :
Of all the noble chargers there they asked the several
    names,
All joyously they sought and heard the names recounted
    o'er ;
While stood King KUSA nigh at hand, as he had stood
    before.

283

He took a clod of earth or dirt that lay behind a horse,
And with it struck the royal Bride upon the back with
    force.
She wrathful grew ; but was appeased, and, as before,
    consoled,
By the sweet, soft, and loving words that unto her were
    told

284

By SĪLAVATI, royal dame, who then returned with
    state
Unto the lordly Palace Tower, and entered through its
    gate,
With her fair daughter, sweet and pure [rare Beauty's
    very flower !]
Nor long did they at rest remain within the Palace
    Tower.

285

When PRABAVATI beautiful, the fount of joy and love,
With form of witching loveliness, like goddesses above,

Told graciously unto the Queen her earnest wish and
    prayer
To see her lord of high desert and graced with merit
    rare !

286

Then said the Queen :—" It is not meet, in our right
    royal race,
For a young Bride [like you, my Own] to see her
    husband's face,
Until she feels a certain hope to bring his throne an
    heir : ". . . .
But while she spoke, the royal Bride paid little heed or
    care !

287

Soon PRABAVATI [came] again, entreated, sought, and
    prayed
To see her husband well-beloved, and tender speeches
    made.
Then did the Queen cause in her heart abundant joy to
    rise,
And lovingly unto the Bride she spoke . . . . and in
    this wise :

288

" Have you good cheer, my daughter dear ! To-morrow
    you will see,
In Sudasuna's lordly street, your spouse of high degree !
Like to the King of Gods above, he bounes him forth
    to ride
On Eravana, beast of state, the elephant of pride ! "

289

Then JAYANPATI did she cause—a handsome prince was he,
Of beauty ever radiant !—adorned with gems to be.

He, young and pleasing ever, was straightway set upon
The grand procession-elephant and on a lofty throne.

290

While Kusa, King of high desert, in poor attire and
    mean,
Like to a groom of elephants in menial post was seen :
Upon the hinder seat he sate—a humble seat and low !
Then, followed by the mighty hosts, they bound them
    forth to go.

291

As roars the sea, the fivefold sorts of music blared and
    blent ;
Into the city on the right the thronged assemblage went !
The window of the Palace Tower aloft was opened
    wide ;
And at the marvellous host looked forth the fair and
    blooming bride.

292

Oh! joyous beat her tender heart to think that happy
    tide—
How good and noble spouse is he who took me for his
    Bride!
The while this chanced, behind the Prince there sat, in
    menial guise,
Shrewd Kusa, who, all-sportive, felt joy in his soul arise.

293

Like well-smoked jaggery very black, or like a big, rough
    cake,
Blackened and burnt and charred all round when it is
    set to bake,

Such was his face, a beardless face, with little nose and
    mean ;
And, wagging to and fro his head, he like a clown was
    seen.

294

Not far the elephant had gone unto another place :
The Queen to PRABAVATI'S side moved but a little space,
And said with loving words to her :—"O fair and
    witching Bride !
Have you a husband meet for you beheld this happy
    tide ? "

295

Much in this fashion, when the Queen had speech and
    question made,
Yet still in PRABAVATI'S heart some doubts and fancies
    weighed :
She said—" Why sat that groom grotesque behind the
    King to-day,
The rude and disobedient lout that made such clownish
    play ? "

296

When PRABAVATI doubtingly her little speech had done :
"'Twas but a groom who there was set to guard
    my royal son,
The King ! "—thus did the stately Queen in ready
    answer say,
Rejoicing much her daughter's mind, and forthwith
    went away.

297

Her who of old had brought her up with tender love
    and warm,
Who still close to her clung, as clings the shadow to
    the form,

[The foster mother], Crooked Dame, she secretly called
   near,
And thus to her in haste she spoke, with loving words
   and dear :

298

"Go thou at once and choose some place [within the
   King's domain],
And, on the royal elephant which beareth riders twain,
Mark and discover which is King—and straightway come
   to me ! "
Then to her Queen the Crooked Dame made thus rejoin-
   der free :

299

"How can I, from the few, few words your Highness
   tells to me,
Discriminate between the two, or which the King may be?
Some other circumstance to name I pray your Highness
   deign ;
And I which of the two is King will straightway ascertain."

300

When phrase by phrase these words she said, the Queen
   replied aloud :—
" Which first from off the elephant descends among the
   crowd
Will be the King: so ascertain and come (as I command)."
Then did the Crooked Dame go forth, and watched and
   took her stand.

301

As is the gem upon the hand right patent to the view,
So inmost thoughts of other men the Lordly One well
   knew :

F

This thing he knew; and hence, because with loving ·
   words he cried,
And pleasant ones—*"Do not reveal this matter to my Bride:"*

302

On that account, the Crooked Dame at once informed the
   Queen :
" With my own eyes the first to light, the Monarch have
   I seen,
From the front seat where he upon the lordly beast did
   ride,
With jewels decked, like SAKRA he, in majesty and
   pride ! "

303

Not few, the false, false words she said.   The Queen
   believed them true ;
For what was falsehood [until then] that Lady never
   knew !
Not doubting that the truth she heard, her heart was
   filled with glee :
She had no fear but of good cheer was she [as Brides
   should be] !

304

Ere long King KUSA, whose deep voice was as a lion's
   roar,
Whose fame was known, by SAKRA shown, to many a
   distant shore,
By glory's fame illustrious, unto the Palace went,
Where dwelt his Mother far renowned, and told her his
   intent.

305

With words ambrosially sweet, he told his wish and
   prayer
All ardent, in the day to see her like a goddess fair,

Queen PRABAVATI, spotless still as is the autumn moon,
And of a gentle nature too—[in wives] a blissful boon !—

306

The Queen, with pleasure hearing this, to answer straight
    began :
" A shrewd device arranging now we severally shall plan.
Rejoice ! Your eyes shall see her well, for, on a coming
    day,
I to the pleasances will bring your Bride and her array."

307

That day went KUSA to the park, and in the pleasance
    pool,
Up to his lips immersed himself in water clear and cool ;
A spreading water-lily leaf upon his head he threw,
And with a blooming lily hid his features all from view.

308

Then was sweet PRABAVATI called to visit the domain ;
Graced was her neck with many a gem and gaud and
    golden chain ;
Apparelled too in soft attire and spotless cloth of gold ;
She was as goddess NANDA was, [the nymph of heavenly
    mould.]

309

That queenly dame, when forth she went with all her
    glad array,
Delighted all the people there who thronged beside the
    way ;
A gentle breeze the bordering trees of sandal softly
    stirred,
Refreshing all the throngs while they the fivefold music
    heard.

310

The women's voices as they sang were like the bees' soft
  hum ;
The music like the cuckoo's notes [from leafy glades that
  come] ;
With fair girl-dancers, like the vines wind-shaken, one
  and all ;
The middle of the pleasance was like KĀMA'S Dancing
  Hall.

311

The cuckoos in the mango-trees, hued like a dark-blue
  cloud,
Sweet mango juice sipped fast and fain—they were a
  noisy crowd : *
Delightful noise it was, in sooth, upon the mangoes
  high,
As if fair PRABAVATI'S praise were uttered in the sky !

312 *

The trees were like to mortal men ; like wives the
  creepers clung ;
The branches shook, but clasped the boughs, as human
  hands the young ;
The tender, budded leaves, like lips ; like mouths, the
  flowers compressed ;
The hum of bees [among the leaves] like hushing babes
  to rest !

313

In rows, nà, champak, mango, jak, and jambu trees were
  near ; *
Amid the boughs the bees' soft hum rejoiced both heart
  and ear;

* See Notes.

Sweet-scented gales the body fanned, and took fatigue
  away:
Who meetly, save ANANTAYA, that park's renown could
  say ?

314

King MADU'S lovely daughter there walked forth and
  merry made,
And plucking many a dainty flower, from place to place
  she strayed ;
Till, when the heat oppressive grew, she wandered to
  the pool,
And with both hands to lave her face, took water clear
  and cool.

315

King KUSA dashed the shading leaf of lily from his
  head,
And boldly then, "*I KUSA am, the handsome King !*" he
  said !
Like to a water-fiend he was, like lion's roar his
  cry !
He seized the Queen's soft, tender arm—he seized and
  held thereby.

316

Now, when that lovely dame beheld that hideous face
  and grim,
Her heart with sorrow's heaped-up flame burnt high. She
  cried to him :
" A monstrous fiend* has seized me now !" with piteous
  voice she said ;
She screamed and sobbed, and many a tear, right bitter
  tears she shed.

* See Notes and the story in the Appendix.

317

Like to a wind-tost golden vine, a creeper slight and slim,
So did her shivering body shake, and trembled every
    limb;
Her face, her eyes with tender hands she hid, as sore
    ashamed,
And, overcome with poignant grief, the hapless dame
    exclaimed :

318

" Upon the cheeks no youthful down or beard is to be
    seen ;
Short, very short, that ill-shaped nose [contemptible and
    mean] ;
The face is like a burnt cake, all blackened, foul, and
    grim ;
A water-fiend, [a gruesome fiend,] is what resembles
    him.

319

" To live and pass my days with him, with him for me to
    share
Whate'er prosperity I may, than that, it better were
That I return, return at once, unto my parents' home ! "
Such was the fixed and firm resolve to which the Bride
    had come.

320

"If, then, King KUSA be the man who clasped in his mine
    arm,
Him hence will I regard as one who still has wrought me
    harm
Throughout from that first day [we went to see the royal
    stud]
Until to-day abiding harm, [but never wrought me
    good !]

321

" True was the utterance of old, of wise men long ago—
Better to choose a single life whose troubles well we know,
Than marriage, where no love may be or joy, to make one's
own !
[And woe is me ! the greatest grief has chanced to me
alone.] "

322

Thus meditating, thereupon she called the brave array
That thither had accompanied her. She sent them not
away :
But straight prepared to journey back unto her distant
home,
The stately city far renowned [whence she betrothed had
come].

323

The Queen, the proud Queen-Mother, heard each circumstance and all ;
And, point by point, of what so soon was likely to
befal,
She to delightful KUSA sent, the King, and let him
know
Immediately [how forth his Bride did boune herself to
go].

324

The King, when he the tidings heard, thus meditating
thought :—
" Should PRABAVATI'S journey now be stayed and come
to nought,
And if of grief her heart shall break, and if of grief she
die,
It will be sad and grievous thing : [I will not her deny !]

325

" However, in the after time, unto our realm again,
With power and glory and renown spread far 'mong
    mortal men,
Here PRABAVATI I shall bring ! Then to the end of
   . time
My fame will ring, and all three worlds will reckon it
    sublime ! "

326

Thus taking heart, and yet with grief, he gave unto the
    dame,
And all the gallant company that thither with her came,
His high consent to journey back unto her native shore.
[And thus the FIFTH PART of our Lay is now recounted
    o'er.]

END OF THE FIFTH PART.

PART VI.

The Departure of Queen Prababati: The History of the Origin of her Dislike to the King.

327

Forth from the city went the Queen, the sweet young
    Queen, once more,
And all the intervening way with haste she travelled
    o'er;
She journeyed on right speedily, and blithely lighted
    down
At SĀGALA, her native place, the city of renown.

328

By ties of love and duty bound—love fond and warmly
    felt—
To both her parents, at their feet, their glorious feet, she
    knelt;
Fair PRABAVATI knelt, and straight with what her heart
    o'erflowed,
Each circumstance and all she told, as she with them
    abode;—

329

How royal KUSA, far renowned, had face so foul and grim

And hideous all; and how her heart felt loathing unto him,

That famous King. Thus did she then each circumstance unfold,

Did PRABAVATI, and the whole unto her parents told.

330

Give ear, O sages, list and learn how chanced that so befel

The destinies of Prince and Bride [which unto you I tell]—

The destinies received for deeds of merit done on earth,

By them, both KUSA and his Bride, while in a former birth.

331

Beside Benares' lordly town, a village was of yore,

A village ever prosperous and decked with plenteous store;

And there two worthy brothers lived, to whom one womb gave birth

[Of modest rural ancestry], but graced with goodly worth.

332

He who was KUSA afterwards was younger of the two,

That worthy twain of brothers. Now, lovely to the view,

And sweet and pleasant ever, a charming damsel there

In that same village did abide, a graceful maid and fair.

333

That dam sel to the elder one had pledged her married
troth,
And been conducted to his home : and all good fortune
both
Attended, while they passed their lives with customs
meet and due,
As might become the worthy line from which descent
they drew.

334

No dwelling had the younger one, so he due honour
paid
Unto his elder brother there, and in his household
stayed.
And thus upon a certain day [now mark the sequel
well,
All ye who listen unto me !] this circumstance befel.

335

Unto the woods the younger went, and, while therein
he stayed,
[The others] toothsome cakes of rice within the dwelling
made:
A part they ate and part they set with thoughtful care
aside,
That he [the absent one] might share when thither home
he hied.

336

Now, in the intervening time, One far renowned came
in,
The PASEMUNI* [who in time to high estate should win].

* See Notes.

He begging came, and thus the dame bestowed with
joyous heart
Upon him then the toothsome cakes that had been set
apart.

337

In fitting mode the cakes he took, upon that day and
place ;
Departing from the household then, he went a little
space,
Not very far; when he, who went within the woods to
roam
[By jungly track], came straightway back, returning to
his home.

338

Then did the dame, who saw, exclaim :—" Count merit
from this day !
To PASEMUNI, fount of bliss, just now I gave away
The portion of the toothsome cakes for you we set apart :
Oh, count the merit [and let joy abound within your
heart] ! "

339

He heard her words, and straightway then he passionately cried :
" Have you twain eaten toothsome cakes, and, what was
set aside,
My portion, given away forsooth ? [A deed, in truth unkind !] "
Thus did he cry, while anger high raged in his heart and
mind.

340

Then off he ran in eager chase : into the begging-bowl
Of PASEMUNI, hands he thrust, [nor could himself control !]

The cakes he snatched from him, on whom they were as
    gifts bestowed ;
And on the self-same spot he stood : [he stood upon the
    road].

341

With her own eyes beholding then what thereupon befel,
The wife rushed straightway from her house, and fast [as
    tongue can tell]
She sought her mother's dwelling-place, and there,
    lamenting sore,
To her with grieving heart [she told] the circumstances
    o'er.

342

A jar of ghee,* fresh, well-preserved, indeed exceeding
    good,
Then did she take and straightway go where PASEMUNI
    stood.
His begging-bowl right well she filled from that capa-
    cious dish ;
And thus the meritorious dame declared her hope and
    wish :

343

" Hereafter, in succeeding births, when I am born again,
Oh, may I spring from lineage high ! That blessing to
    me deign
To grant, I pray, so that I may be sweet and fair to see,
The daughter of a lofty line, and not of low degree !

344

" And spotless like the autumn moon, in majesty and
    grace,
Grant that to me may be assigned a sweet and lovely face,

* See Notes.

One that shall scatter beams of light all radiantly
    abroad
[A face that men shall love to see, and gather round, and
    laud].

345

" Like to a heavenly goddess fair, all radiantly may I
Take still in thrall and bind to me beholder's heart and
    eye !
With goodly beauty well endowed, O be the portion
    mine,
With all prosperity and joy for ever more to shine !

346

" Remote from haunts of wicked men may I remain afar;
But ever friendly be to those that good and virtuous
    are.
Deep in my heart may virtue be, and wisdom, boons of
    mine,
And to my family may I with lamp-like lustre shine !

347

" Like fragrance of both sandal woods, O be such fra-
    grance mine,
Proceeding from my graceful form [delightful, sweet,
    divine],
And like the scent of lotus flowers [that glow through
    all the South],
Be ever the sweet, dainty breath of my delicious mouth!"

348

Thus did she wish, and thereupon a fit obeisance made,
And, kneeling down, unto the feet due adoration paid,—

The feet of him with attributes of rarest merit graced :
Then up she rose and at one side herself the damsel
placed.

349

Now he who had the rice-cakes snatched from
PASEMUNI'S hand,
Did close beside, and on the spot, the whole beholding,
stand.
The scene with his own eyes he saw, and all that there
occurred,
[And knew right well] the lofty wish the damsel had
preferred.

350

To PASEMUNI straight he went, and unto Him again
The toothsome cakes he took away he offered fast and
fain.
And straight preferred an ardent wish (with fervour
worshipping
And love) that from that goodly deed a fivefold fruit
might spring.

351

[And said :] " By the transcendent sheen of this high
deed of worth,
Hereafter may it chance to me, in some succeeding
birth,
That I receive of might and fame a great and goodly
store,
And reign the sovereign King of all on DAMBADIVA'S
shore !

352

" With glory and magnificence and majesty endowed,
Like to the roar of lions may my voice be strong and
loud,

And forth proceeding from my mouth in all directions
fly,
And pierce and far resounding go to all points of the
sky !

353

"This dame, with radiant beauty graced, however far
she be,
E'en though a hundred yoduns * off, though sundered
then from me,
Grant that to me she may be brought with power [and
pride serene],
And share my lofty throne with me, my consort and my
Queen."

354

Thus by the meritorious deeds they wrought it did
occur :
According to the prayers preferred, it chanced to him and
her,
And PRABAVATI afterwards [endowed with magic grace],
And princely KUSA, far renowned, were born of royal
race.

355

Know ye, O sages, that the face of KUSA was so grim
And hideously foul, because he took the cakes from Him,
High PASEMUNI, angrily, with passion hot and high
[Such deeds of passion never may pass unrequited by].

356

Moreover, know with certainty, the loathing that did
spring,
In PRABAVATI'S heart towards [her lordly spouse] the
King,

* See Notes.

King KUSA, high-renowned, arose from that far day of
    old
When [how she still might loathe him much] her wish
    the damsel told.

357

As certainly as if to heaven a pebble you may throw,
There will it not abide at all, but fall to earth below ;
So, well-proportioned to your deeds, or be they good or ill.
Will the event your hearts desire be meted to you still ! *

END OF THE SIXTH PART.

---

* See Notes. This stanza embodies a leading Buddhistic dogma,
and may be pronounced the moral of the book.

PART VII.

King Kusa's Lament and Pursuit.

358

That day when PRABAVATI left, departing for her home
With all her retinue, sore grief did to her husband come:
As when at eve the golden sun slides down the glowing
    west,
The closing rays the lilies close, [and give the blossoms
    rest !]

359

The Sun is husband to the West, and unto her he goes,
And leaves behind a grieving Spouse, the Pond where
    lotus blows !
She folds the fingers of her hands, like lotus petals gay,
And like to rings and gems the strings of bees she flings
    away !

360

The radiance of the bright, full Moon made glad the
    Milky Main ;
In many a place around was heard the cuckoo's gladsome
    strain ;
The gentle wind the pollen kissed, and scattered it afar :
Then KĀMA, waging contest high, did boune him forth
    to war !

361

The BŌDISAT, who was the King, upon his couch alone
Erelong reclined, while in his mind keen sorrow fixed
    her throne,—
Sorrow the sorest that could be, because his bride was
    flown,
Fair PRABAVATI, ever dear, who like a goddess shone!

362

King KUSA, whose ambrosial words could highest joy
    impart,
Of high desert, found anguish grow unceasing in his
    heart :
All sleepless he [upon his couch the midnight silence
    broke],
And thus his woeful, sad lament the grieving Monarch
    spoke :

363

" My palace halls are empty all, since forth my Bride
    would go !
Nor song nor dance of maidens now on me can joy
    bestow !
The flowers that deck our bridal-bed are thorns arrayed
    in rows !
The Moon is like the Sun that beams upon a kalpa's *
    close !

364

" When shall I clasp my Own again, or lay me by her
    side ?
[My Own, my brightly beautiful, my Darling and my
    Bride !]

        * See Notes.

Her face was like the blossomed flowers upon the golden
    vines,
A rare sweet face of magic grace, where soft light ever
    shines!

365

"No more the Moon beams cool and mild, but like the
    Sun she burns;
The pleasant song the cuckoo chants to yells of demons
    turns!
How shall my heart sweet solace find, how quell this
    anguish sore,
Since PRABAVATI, best-beloved, abides with me no more?

366

"My PRABAVATI, best-beloved, like to a crystal pool!
Her breasts, the snowy swans that glide upon the water
    cool;
Her eyes, blue lotus; eyebrows, bees; her face, a lily
    fair;
When shall I fondly clasp my love, with joy beyond
    compare?"

367

When PRABAVATI left him lone and far away had gone,
O how shall I describe the woe of him, that Lordly
    One!
Who, with fit attributes endowed, in time should BUDDHA
    be,
And rescue all men from the strifes of Life's tempestuous
    sea!

368

With dance and song the girlish throng, a beautiful array,
Sought variously to soothe the King, and drive his grief
    away;

But, failing in whate'er they tried, calm, still, and silent all,
They stood as stand the painted forms that grace a frescoed wall !

369

Thus did the Sun-descended King, of high renown and rare,
Spend that drear night, which seemed as if a kalpa * long it were :
At last, unclosing garden-plots, where bright the lily blows,
Within the rosy eastern sky, the golden Sun arose.

370

*　　*　　*　　*　　*　　*

[This stanza in the original is considered spurious. It is unfit for translation.]

371

[Such was the night ; but] at the dawn, the cheerful dawn of day,
The Lordly One bethought himself:—"Hence will I speed away
To SĀGALA [the stately town on MADURATA'S shore],
And hither PRABAVATI bring unto my home once more.

372

"Until, my objects all achieved, I seek my realm again,
And spread abroad my name and might through all the tribes of men,

* See note to stanza 246.

The city's welfare and the state's to guard and keep in
    trust,
It well befits me to provide arrangements meet and just.

373

" Now if I give that royal trust unto my sire, the King,
Or brother [JAYANPATI], it will be parlous thing
And difficult to take it back, when I shall claim my
    own ;
[For he that once the sceptre sways is loth to leave the
    throne."]

374

So entering straight the Palace Tower, where did the
    Queen abide,
His Mother, he saluted her, and, standing at one side
[As reverent sons should ever do], he thus with her con-
    ferred,
And forthwith said full many a sweet and many a
    courteous word.

375

" Like to a city of the gods by gallant army held,
An army thoroughly equipped [which foe hath never
    quelled],
Is KUSĀVATI, this fair town of ours, my Mother dear ;
And all the wealth and bravery we see collected here,

376

" Take you in charge and government, till back I bring
    again
[The peerless bride who left my side with all her gallant
    train],

Queen PRABAVATI [best beloved : this is my wish to-
day] ! "
Thus did he with auspicious words unto the Lady say.

377

The Queen, his Mother, heard the speech : She found he
would not stay,
Though woman's wiles she tried indeed his going to delay.
But finding that of no avail, provisions she prepared,
Sweet food and fitted for the road, when forth on it he
fared.

378

The victuals in a golden dish she placed, and in the
hand
Of him, the Lordly One, to whom she gave this last
command :
" Go now, and come again to me with fortune good and
fair ! "
And said a loving, fond farewell, since forth he sought
to fare.

379

Then to the Queen, his Mother, there he salutation
paid ;
With plenteous love and reverence a meet obeisance
made ;
And bowing low [as children should, who filial duty
prize],
Unto the Queen he straightway spoke, he spoke, and in
this wise :

380

"O my sweet Lady Mother dear! if prosperous I re-
　main,
Returning speedily to you, I you shall see again!"
So did he speak unto the Queen, then to his chamber
　he
Went straightway, where his bed was placed, a glorious
　room to see.

381

With weapons five he armed himself, right well equipped
　and graced;
Of gold a thousand pieces next within a bag he placed;
And, last of all, the gay guitar of melody so rare,
He took unto his royal hand, and bound him forth to
　fare.

382

He left the city far behind; and, while 'twas early day,
Full half-a-hundred yoduns* he had sped upon his way,
Then [lighting down upon the ground, for he, though
　nerved with steel,
Could feel the pangs of hunger too] dispatched his mid-
　day meal.

383

The fifty yoduns that remained with speed he travelled
　o'er,
And reached the town of SĀGALA [on MADURATA'S
　shore].
Ere evening had arrived that day, he stood within the
　town
[So rapid was the journey made by him of high renown].

* See note to stanza 353.

384

Now,. at that time the stately Queen, fair PRABAVATI sweet,

Had just arisen and stood beside her own accustomed scat,

The influence of the Lordly One, all glorious and divine,

Made her to shake and tremble like the trembling golden vine !

END OF THE SEVENTH PART.

PART VIII.

—◇—

What King Kusa Underwent at Sāgala.

385

The Lordly One, the Chief of Earth, went down the
    crowded street,
Alighting there; and one, well-pleased, his coming then
    did greet,
An aged woman [who abode within a lowly home];
For weariness was on his frame and unto him had come.

386

She called to him indoors to go; upon a goodly seat
She caused him at that time to sit; and then upon his
    feet—
Upon his feet her hands at once affectionately she placed,
With joy and love [thus did the dame to him with
    merit graced].

387

Then for the Bōdisat did she prepare delicious meat,
And rice and curry savoury, and made him of them eat;
Right palatable food it was, made by that ancient dame,
Who [garrulous and] glad of heart immediately became.

388

Then did the Lordly One take out the thousand coins of
gold
And golden dish [right costly gifts and glorious to
behold],
And gave them to the ancient dame, whose heart with
praise ran o'er
[And gratitude to own and take such rare and precious
store] !

389

According to his wish, he placed the steely weapons five
Within the house to keep them safe [thus did the Lord
contrive] ;
And saying—" On a journey now behoves me to begone,"
He took the gay guitar in hand, of sweet, melodious
tone.

390

The stables of the elephants, among the stable-folk,
He entered next, and winning words and pleasant ones
he spoke ;
[And thus he said]—" O if a place on me is here be-
stowed,
For me 'twill be a resting-place, a lodging, and abode !

391

" On my guitar of melody rare music will I make,
That in your hearts profound delight ineffable will
wake ! "
Then all the grooms assembled there, with joyous heart
and mind,
To him a place and truss of grass with readiness
assigned.

392

All joyfully upon the ground the grass he duly spread,
A little bundle of the same he put beneath his head :
A while he slept, and then he rose. ˙ The slumber drove from him,   .
In part, the heavy weariness [that seized on nerve and limb].

393

He lifted up his gay guitar, he struck sweet notes right soon,
And forthwith waked melodiously a rare and thrilling tune,
Like to the choirs of heaven on high. He played so sweet and clear,
That all within the city walls the melody might hear.

394

Queen PRABAVATI at that time upon her bed reclined,
She heard the music floating in [as floats the summer wind] !
A while as to the sound she mused :—" Celestial airs they are,
But not from other's lute they come, save one well-known guitar.

395

" King KUSA, bravely gifted one, in search of me [I know]
Has hither come to this domain : [it must, it must be so !
For but from his guitar alone could flow that melting strain."]
Thus having settled in her mind, she laid her down again.

396

King MADU said [as he, too, heard the music from afar] :
" To-morrow morning will I hear the sound of that
    guitar."
But [ere the morn] the Lordly One far from that place
    had sped,
And eaten food at the abode [the old dame's lowly
    shed].

397

The Lordly One a Potter saw, the chief one in the
    town,
[Who doubtless had in his degree no small or slight re-
    nown ;]
Chief Potter he, and goodly store of pitchers he sup-
    plied
Unto the · Palace.   Thus to him beseechingly he
    cried :

398

" O sir ! if near you I might live, I would devote my
    days
In moulding pitchers beautiful, the cause of joy and
    praise,"
He said : [so winningly he spoke, persuasively and well,
That from the Potter] he received permission there to
    dwell.

399

[With diligence from early morn, the very break of day]
Until the sun the zenith reached, he brought and kneaded
    clay,
He sat him down to mould the shapes of pitchers fair
    and gay,
And whirled his potter's wheel about, without or stop or
    stay.

400

Right brilliant figures did he paint, still thinking in his
    soul,
"Soon will I PRABAVATI see;" and many a noble bowl,
And chatty large and small and round, and fit for vari-
    ous use,
Did he, the Lordly One, with care and cunning skill
    produce.

401

He baked unto the proper heat, and brought them forth
    to view:
They pleased the Potter mightily, whose joy increasing
    grew.
He tied them in a pingo load,* he tied the vessels all,
And straightway with them went he forth unto the
    Palace Hall.

402

Now, when he showed them to the King, the Monarch
    cried with glee:
"Who made these royal pitchers fair, O Potter tell to
    me?
Well shaped and moulded splendidly, in manner fit and
    fair
[There never yet was pitcher made that could with these
    compare]!"

403

Unto the words the King vouchsafed, the Craftsman
    thus replied:
"The man who moulded these, O Sire, doth now with
    me abide!
A servant under me he lives, and meetly has he done
The pitchers he was set to make, right nobly every one!"

* See Notes.

404

The King the answer heard [and thus :—" So cunning is
his skill],
The post of teacher unto you right meetly may he fill !
Now see the gold [I give to thee] to him give every
part ;
And say to him, all reverently, *O teach to me mine art !* "

405

A thousand pieces broad of gold unto the Potter then
He caused to be bestowed, and filled his heart with joy
again.
Then said :—" These pitchers meetly made, we do command this day
Unto our daughters to be given, that they therewith may
play ! "

406

Obedient to the King's command, the Potter took his
wares,
And to the daughters of the throne distributed in
shares.
Now this befel [the truth I tell] by virtue of the will
Of him, the Lordly One [renowned for matchless power
and skill].

407

Now he, when he the pitchers formed, so excellent and
fair,
Had painted on their rounded sides, with colours bright
and rare,
The features of the Lordly One, fair PRABAVATI'S shape,
And marks upon the Crooked Dame : [not one he let
escape.]

408

When thus the pitchers had been given to PRABAVATI's
    view,
She fixed on them her eyes and straight right well the
    maker knew,
The Lordly One: and she exclaimed :—"No need of
    these have I !
Throw them away this very day!" [thus did the Lady
    cry.]

409

Moreover, thus she cried :—"Bestow on any one you
    please
The pitchers [hither brought, I say : I need not such as
    these] !"
Then did her seven sisters all begin to vex and tease
Her [for young girls occasion meet to plague will ever
    seize !]

410

"Oh ! is it then your lofty Spouse who made these
    pitchers rare,
King KUSA, far-renowned, and shaped them all with
    cunning care ?"
Though much their speech annoyed her heart, she kept
    her secret well,
And of the bitter, bitter facts no tittle did she tell.

411

He whom the King had favoured so, the Potter, straight
    went home,
And, carrying gold, with hasty steps did to his dwelling
    come.

Then to the Lordly One he gave the thousand coins of
    gold
[And everything that had occurred with speed he
    straightway told].

412

Now when the gold to him was given, King KUSA, sweet
    and good,
Thus musing thought :—" If here I stay [it will not work
    me good] ;
Nor will I PRABAVATI see [the dame of beauty rare ;
No longer will I here remain, but other venture dare "].

413

To one who wove of rushy reeds fair fans and such like
    ware
He went, and straight engaged himself ; and, living with
    him there,
[Did all such work as appertains unto that lowly art :]
In all the master made and wrought, as servant he took
    part.

414

Thence to a Weaver of fair wreaths and gay festoons of
    flowers,
He went, and straightway won his heart [so witching
    were his powers] ;
And there he dwelt, and garlands wove, no little stock
    or store
And as the Craftsman lived, so he the weary days out-
    wore.

415

Now, know ye that, as he had done when with the
    Potter, he
Abode and at his house, so still, and in a like degree

H

And manner, did he ever act [with others when he dwelt ;
And like results did he achieve—and longing sore he
felt].

416

King KUSA, graced with glory's blaze, went thus from
spot to spot,
Still longing to behold the Queen—and yet beheld her
not.
Not winning what he so desired, sore grief and trouble
fell
On him [that great and glorious King, whose miseries I
tell].

417

At last he from the Palace Cook some favour did obtain
(The Cook who served King MADU'S food and cleared
away again);
And well-behaving unto him, within the cooking-place
Of that high palace he abode ; and thus he passed his
days. . . .

418

Following the gastronomic rules * laid down for every-
thing
[For sauce and soup and every dish], unto that lordly
King.
Great joy was caused by banquets rich, as if for gods'
array ;
Rare food, indeed, was thus prepared : and on a certain
day,

419

The Palace Cook a pingo took of rice, with care prepared,
And straightway to the Palace Hall right speedily he
fared.

* See Notes.

The Monarch finished his repast in order meet and due,
And joy [which after dinner comes] within his bosom
grew.

420

Now, at that tide, the Lordly One took sundry scraps of
meat,
With bones all mixed, and cooked it straight so savoury
and so sweet,
It tasted like ambrosial food, and such delicious reek
It sent abroad [as men would laud, and high encomium
speak].

421

The King sniffed up the savoury scent, and question
thus made he :
" What other food, what other food may in the Kitchen
be,
Within the Palace Kitchen now?" for, pleasing him
right well,
That stately Monarch had inhaled the rare, delicious
smell.

422

[The Cook replied :]—" In order, Sire, thy menials all
may eat,
One of my helpers under me hath gathered scraps of meat,
Some scraps of meat well mixed with bones, and, cooking
them with care,
Doth for his fellow-servants now a savoury meal prepare ! "

423

The King, when he the words had heard, thus mused
within his mind :
" No doubt it is ambrosial food, and fitting praise should
find ! "

He said :—"[Now to the Kitchen] haste as quickly as
    you can,
And hither bring that [savoury food to glad mine inner
    man]!"

424

All rapidly then went he down, and brought the savoury
    food,
And gave it to the lofty King [who straight pronounced
    it good].
Right fond of it the Monarch grew, and in his mouth he
    placed
With joy the sweet, delicious food [that gratified the
    taste].

425

The palate's seven hundred nerves the rare sensation
    fleet
Conveyed through all the Monarch's frame—he over-
    flowed with sweet :
With savoury, sweet deliciousness the Monarch over-
    flowed,
And thus did he address [the Cook, who in the hall
    abode] :

426

"These thousand coins of gold with haste give to him
    when you go,
Upon his genius rare and fine encomiums high bestow !
Hereafter, from this very day, let him our food prepare—
[The food our royal house consumes—right royal, dainty
    fare] !

427

"The food so cooked, bring thou to us ; but to our
    daughters fair
[The eight princesses beautiful that bless a father's care,

Henceforth] let him convey the food, [right sweet and
    dainty fare !]"
Thus did the Monarch to the Cook his royal will declare.

428

Unto the Lordly One he went, and gave unto his hand
The thousand coins of gold, of gold, and told the King's
    command :
The circumstances each and all he told unto him then,
While joy increased within the heart [of KUSA, King of
    men] !

429

When he received the thousand coins, the thousand coins
    of gold,
Within his heart great joy arose, serene and manifold :
And having won one object sought, thus did he commune
    then :
" Now will mine eyes the Lady see, [and greet mine Own
    again !] "

430

Thus thought the Lordly One renowned. Sleep's langour
    he undid :
Before the dawn of day he rose [ere yet the sun had slid
Above the eastern hills], he rose, and in a savoury wise
Rare rice and curry did he cook—[the standing dish we
    prize] !

431

Unto the Master Cook he gave the dishes for the King ;
But for the fair Princesses there the share apportioning,
He made into a pingo-load, and shouldered it with care
[And unto the zenana straight did he with joy repair].

432

Like to a cook, with body daubed with soot and dirt and
   grime,
Appeared the BŌDISAT, and came upon that very time
Unto the fair zenana's door, the rooms where did abide
Queen PRABAVATI [well-beloved, the queen of grace and
   pride].

433

The Queen, when she beheld him there [thought then
   this very thing]:
"King KUSA, DAMBADIVA'S lord, of all the sovereign
   King,
Has hither come for love of me [far from his realm and
   home:
Such is the longing he endures that tempts him far to
   roam].

434

"And slavish toil, unmeet for him [the son of ancient
   kings,
He now performs], and wearily a load of dishes brings :
Therefore, if even for a time, I harsh rebuke forego,
And from my mouth let no reproof or indignation flow,

435

"Such is the love within his heart, the fervid love for
   me,
Reflecting [on my silence] then, no more, no more will
   he
To any other place repair, but only here abide
[*For best the heart delights to dwell, where those it loves
   abide*]!

436

"So, if I use him vilely now, and speak harsh words
    that pain
His soul, I shall induce him straight to seek his realm
    again,
Unto his realms again to go." Thus did the Queen de-
    vise
Within her mind : and then she spoke—she spoke, and
    in this wise :

437

"O Kusa, lofty King and Lord ! You have forsaken all
Your fair possessions that are bound by Kusāvatī's
    wall,
And hither to this town have come, and menial service
    done,
Unfit and unbecoming toils, and slavish every one.

438

"Why do you bear this misery, why choose with cooks
    to dwell,
By night and day the fuel bring, and water from the
    well,
And cook and carry many a dish in loads [as servants
    do]?
Why do you bear this slavish life,—what boots it unto
    you?

439

"You, who an ugly face possess, a face like to a cake
All charred and burnt, should for your Queen and royal
    Consort take
A woman like a female fiend [a loathly dame to see,
That so the Lord and Bride might both be equal in de-
    gree]!

440

" And go with her unto your town, your town of glory
　　rare,
Famed KUSĀVATI, far renowned, and living with her
　　there,
Enjoy all fair prosperity !　Here do not longer stay
Within this city, I desire !　Hear, menial, what I say !

441

" How long soever you remain, O Lord of ugly face !
How many days soe'er you choose to hold abiding-place
Here in this stately town of ours [this truth accept from
　　me],
That I shall ever live with you, can never, never be !

442

"So go your way from hence, I pray, to KUSĀVATI'S
　　town
[The city of your lordly realm, the city of renown] ! "
Unto the words, the bitter words, the queenly Dame had
　　said,
Then in this wise the Lordly One therewith rejoinder
　　made :

443

" O you who charm men's eyes and hearts, whose ever-
　　radiant hair,
Dark, dark blue like a cloud, and long and soft and
　　thick and rare,
With face all gloriously fair, like to the Moon on high,
When full [in argent loveliness she walks athwart the
　　sky] !

444

" O PRABAVATI ! beautiful, right lovely, radiant one !
Your breasts, your soft, round, swelling breasts, are like
  unto the swan !
Your slender waist, your dainty waist, has grown so
  slim and slight
As if from bearing up the weight of breasts so full and
  bright !

445

" If it be granted unto me at all times to behold
Your beauty sweet and rare, the joy a hundred thousand-
  fold
Will far exceed the plenteous fame, the heavenly high
  renown   .
That flourishes in the gods' abode, the proud celestial
  town !

446

" Now is the darkness blinding deep of the strong love
  [I bore
And bear] that binds me unto you, that binds for ever-
  more.
I cannot see my way to go, the way I cannot see,
And thus to KUSĀVATI'S town the road is not for me !

447

" If I might have the precious boon your beauty still to
  see,
That loveliness right beautiful [and O so dear to me !]
The rich possessions I enjoy within my royal home,
I would not value—not so much as one poor drop of
  foam ! "

448

Then PRABAVATI when she heard, [thought :]—"If the
    glorious King,
Great KUSA, seize upon my hand, there is not anything
Or person in the world who may the hardy deed prevent
[So mused the dame, nor did the thought yield unto
    her content].

449

Thus meditating, straight she closed the palace-chamber
    door,
And laid her on her glorious couch, her couch all shining
    o'er,
Like to a goddess [from on high, right beautiful to see !
Than PRABAVATI, fairer dame on earth may never be].

450

The Lordly One upon that tide took up the pingo-load,
Unto the seven royal dames with it in haste he strode ;
The service then required of him he failed not to dis-
    charge,
Then cleared away the dishes all, both little ones and
    large.

451

When out of that a part was given to PRABAVATI fair,
Unto the Crooked Dame she gave her own peculiar
    share,
And what the Crooked One received, her portion duly set,
The queenly dame took to herself, took to herself and
    ate.

452

She warned the Crooked Dame and said :—"[O foster-
    mother dear !]
Tell not to any one, the King, the glorious King is here ;

King KUSA to this town has come on my account alone :
[I would not have the circumstance to any one made
    known !] "

453

No other person save the Queen and her, the Crooked
    One,
Knew the delightful Lordly One renowned had thither
    gone
[To that high town had gone, the town endowed with
    splendour rare],
And there abode and lived and dwelt, [a prey to grief
    and care].

454

While thus he spent the weary days, the Lordly One did
    see
Queen PRABAVATI at the bath, the dame of high degree.
The pain of love and fire of grief his bosom tortured
    sore,
Great tortures [that might well consume the bosom's in-
    most core] !

455

Then [said or thought] the Lordly One, upon a certain
    tide—
"Now will I make experiment, and know if she, my
    Bride,
Queen PRABAVATI, has for me, or not, love in her breast ;
Thus will I learn with certainty, and set my doubts at
    rest."

456

Rice he prepared, and took it straight to the princesses
    rare,
The lovely seven, and service wrought in manner fit
    and fair.

The service done, he tied his load [of dishes then and
    there],
And, shouldering it, [right speedily he from the hall did
    fare.]

457

In divers places, as he went, he tripped and stumbled
    sore,
He rubbed his feet upon the ground, and pressed them
    on the floor;
At length, at PRABAVATI's door, the Queen's door, down
    he fell,
And, tumbling on the earth, he lay and groaned, and
    groaned right well.

458

The Queen that circumstance beheld [and said] :—" For
    me alone
What misery the Lord endures of DAMBADIVA's throne,
King KUSA, prince of all [the earth, a very King of
    Kings,
Endures [and slavishly submits unto the meanest things]!

459

" Now, if he enter to this place, and die upon this time,
Perchance, to take my life away will not be deemed a
    crime ! "
[So, that she might escape the chance of that unwelcome
    doom,]
She thought of it a second time, and went from out her
    room.

460

Then as she came, that charming Dame bent low that
    she might see,
And trembled sore, to ascertain if yet the life might be

Within the Bōdisat, the great; she shook and trembled
    sore,
As earnestly she looked and bent his prostrate body o'er.

461

The mouth of him the Bōdisat, the great, was filled
    with foam;
And then a drop, a frothing drop, he straightway made
    to come
Upon fair PRABAVATI'S face, that sweet and lovely flower
[That had of perfect loveliness a transcendental dower].

462

The Queen arose, and straight returned unto her chamber,
    then
She closed the door a little way, and thus she spoke
    again—
Right bitter and vexatious words she spoke, and in this
    wise
[As she within the chamber stood, while wrath gleamed
    from her eyes] :

463

" If ever one of ugly face, if such a bridegroom, sought
A beauteous woman for his wife, to him whenever
    aught
Of fate or fortune chanced to him, save lucklessness and
    woe !
[Such has it ever been on earth : it ever will be so.]

464

" Two iron fragments, save, indeed, with heat they *both*
    shall glow,
Together ne'er will welded be ; and, in like manner, so

Two beings never can unite whose love is not the same,
[Who feel no glow within their hearts of one affection's
  flame.]

465

"O you, of ugliness possessed, who seek and long for
  me—
A thing unmeet—hereafter now a goodly thing 'twill
  be
If where we severally shall dwell be kept asunder far
[That we may never meet again, we twain, who sundered
  are].

466

"Then here, I pray, no longer stay, abide you here no
  more,
Not even for a little while, but seek the distant shore
Where stands proud KUSĀVATĪ'S town, the city rich and
  fair."
Thus spoke to him the royal Dame—[she spoke with
  angry air].

467

That Being, when these facts he heard, nor vexed nor
  wrathful grew,
Not even a little in his heart, for love had made him
  true,
And bound him to the royal dame : and thus he made
  reply
To her, and in the following words [as she was standing
  by]:

468

"Even when your anger waxes hot, with joy our bosoms
  swell
The more—[you are so beautiful that all becomes you
  well];

Our joy increases then, just as the wreathing flowers
will blow
When scathingly the sun's bright rays with heat in-
tensest glow!

469

" Here if I stay, your loveliness and beauty's pride I
see ;
Your sweet, enchanting words I hear, for ever dear to
me ;
Though other joys may ne'er be mine, still *these* will joy
bestow
Upon my heart, as here I stay : *I cannot, cannot go !*

470

" Not to a distance will I go, but here will I remain,
And pass my days within this town, and this beloved
domain."
Thus did the BŌDISAT resolve—a resolution high,
And thus he straight informed the Queen [as she was
standing by].

471

The Queen, when she the answer heard [thought thus
within her heart] :
"Forth from this place will I see well that he shall soon
depart ! "
With shrewdness, then, within her heart a scheme she
did devise ;
And thereupon the royal Dame rejoined, and in this
wise :

472

" The toils and troubles you endure, while here you do
remain,
Result in constant weariness and fruitless, bitter pain :

You might as well endeavour now to catch the fleeting
    wind
Within a net—the fleeting breeze, that never was con-
    fined !

473

" For you to wait so long, so long, enduring woe and
    pain,
And seek to win me for your own, whom you shall ne'er
    obtain,
Is just as if a famished crane, that food was needing
    sore,
Should wait until the sea dried up, upon the sandy
    shore ! "

474

Thus when such cruel, bitter words had said that queenly
    Dame,
Then did the mighty Bōdisat all prayerfully exclaim—
Being bound by love to her, and held in its enclasping
    thrall—
He straightway spoke, and these the words the Bōdisat
    let fall :

475

" The royal wealth and stately pride of Dambadiva
    high,
Nor small indeed that regal state, forsaking, hither I,
For love of you, for love of you, for you alone, I came ;
And here have I remained so long, O peerless queenly
    Dame !

476

" From you, so rare and radiant still, no sidelong glance,
    not one,
From forth the corner of your eye on me has ever shone !

Not e'en one little loving word have I received from
    you—
A boon that would have joyed my heart with pleasure
    fond and true !

477

" When one of these I shall receive, right joyous shall I
    be,
As if far-spreading royal state were then bestowed on
    me !
Then shall I go, as you desire ; but, if I ne'er receive,
Until my life departs from me, this realm *I will not
leave !* "

478

Thus did he speak ; and thereupon the Queenly Dame
    replied,
And falsely too * [but, first of all, unto herself she cried],
Thinking indeed :—" Ere long, ere long shall I see to 't
    with care,
And forth departing hence right soon shall I behold him
    fare."

479

" O Sire and Lord of Earth ! I called—it was not long
    ago—
A throng of wise astrologers, who may the future know,
And then from them this circumstance I sought [with
    ardour keen],
If it was fated I should live your Consort and your
    Queen.

480

" Thus, when I asked them, they replied :—' It never will
    be so ;
With that high King you ne'er will live, nor e'er with
    him will go ;

* See Notes.

I

Not even though your body were, with sharp division
    keen,
In seven pieces cut and hacked ! You ne'er will be his
    Queen ! '

481

" Because that was the speech they made, because of
    what I saw
Of other things, I never will, while life's dear breath I
    draw,
Abide with you—with you, who own a face so foul and
    grim ! "
[Such was the speech the Queenly Dame therewith
    addressed to him.]

482

Unto the utterance of the Queen the Lordly One re-
    plied,
And in this wise :—" Beloved One, my darling and my
    pride!
I also called astrologers, the fortune-telling train,
And questions, ere I came away, I asked of them full
    fain.

483

"[They said :] ' *The stately Queenly Dame all glorious to
the view,*
Sweet PRABAVATI, *never may have other spouse than you !* '
O therefore now abandon straight the hardness that you
    bear
To me, that cruel, harsh resolve, O PRABAVATI fair !

484

" If unto me you ever look with eyes like lotus blue,
And give a soft and tender glance—a glance to thrill me
    through ;

And if on me a little smile you ever shall bestow,
Or fitly speak a loving word, *then* quickly will I go.

485

"Then quickly will I go indeed. But if in such a
    wise
No grace on me shall be conferred [from lips or beam-
    ing eyes],
Then will I service as a cook perform, and here abide ! "
Thus spoke he [all-resolvèd then, unto his peerless
    Bride].

486

Now when the Lordly One spoke thus, the Dame made
    answer free,
Sweet PRABAVATI, when she heard:—"It matters nought
    to me,
Or if this person goes or stays ! For him have I no
    care,
[Whether he in the town abides, or forth from it shall
    fare."]

487

Thus meditating, forth did she unto her chamber fare,
And shut with force the heavy bolts the door that guarded
    there ;
And mounted then her glorious couch, her couch so rich
    and rare,
And like a goddess there reposed, [that radiant Queen
    and fair.]

488

This circumstance did he behold—with his own eyes he
    saw ;
While storms of anguish smote his heart, [his heart with-
    out a flaw.]

Upon his shoulder he upraised his heavy slavish load,
And to the Palace Kitchen thence all-sorrowfully strode.

489

For love, for very love alone, these services he wrought :
He kept the fires from going out ; the water too he
  brought
With his own hands ; and pitchers washed and turned
  them up to dry ;
And in the morning first he rose, [ere dawn blushed o'er
  the sky.]

490

And in the morning, cakes he made and conjy [for the
  rest,
At dawn ;] and night and day cooked rice and curry of
  the best ;
And beverages, luscious ones, and sweets did he prepare ;
And tied up pingo loads of these with readiness and
  care.

491

And took the loads and bore them fast to the Princesses
  all,
Performing service for those dames, obedient to their
  call,
From day to day. The BŌDISAT, while there he did
  abide,
Felt sorrow's fire within his soul [keep maddening him
  beside].

492

Now, did the Lordly One behold, upon a certain day,
The Crooked Dame come from the room where PRA-
  BAVATI lay,

The Palace Chamber painted fair.   He called her to his
 side,
And unto her he spoke these words, upon that very
 tide :

493

" Go forth unto your Queenly Dame, and bow before her
 there,
Sweet PRABAVATI beautiful, whose glory may compare
With LAKSHMI'S all divine and bright, and straight to
 her declare
The misery and sore distress which I all-vainly bear !

494

" And if, from what you shall devise, hereafter I shall
 meet
From PRABAVATI, beautiful, illustrious, and sweet,
A tender glance, delicious all, a glance to thrill me
 through,
Or loving utterance or word, [now, mark what I shall
 do !]

495

" The day to KUSĀVATI'S town I shall return and go,
O proud and happy shall you be ; for I will make you
 so
As if your crookedness were fled ! I shall embellish you
With priceless gems and jewels rare, and rich gauds not
 a few ! "

496

When this the Lordly One had said, the Crooked Dame
 with joy
Delicious to the chamber went, the Palace Hall thereby :

In haste she went [and robed herself in vesture fair and
    gay],
And swept away all filth and dirt, without the least
    delay.

497

With loving words she called the Dame, the Queenly
    Dame so fair,
Sweet PRABAVATI beautiful, and set her on a chair,
A lowly chair or seat it was, while she, [the Crooked
    One,]
Another and a loftier seat straight placed herself upon.

498

She loosed the Queen's thick jetty locks, the tresses long
    and soft,
And with her fingers smoothed them all, she rubbed and
    pressed them oft.
She took an insect from her head, she did, that Crooked
    Dame,
And put it on the Queen's fair head—[it was a deed to
    blame !]

499

Then out she took it straight again, and in the hand she
    laid
Of her, the lovely Queen :—"See what an insect huge has
    strayed
Upon your head so delicate, your shining, winsome
    head !"
[Thus did she speak, and then she paused]: and then
    again she said :

500

" Unto this city One has come, and dwelleth here alone,
King KUSA, of the Solar line the pinnacle ! yea, One

Whose lovely, flower-like feet are set upon the heads of
  kings,
Of kings in DAMBADIVA'S realms, [the first of earthly
  things.]

501

" For some time now has he abode among the kitchen
  crew,
That, fired with earnest love and fond, he oft might look
  on you.
Among the cooks he lives and works, a life of toil and
  care,
And every day, and all day long, sore anguish doth he
  bear.

502

" With him but once his couch to share a tender spouse
  and true,
And drive his weariness away, how many dames, save
  you,
How many a dame throughout the world, would aim and
  strive with joy,
To drive the trouble from his heart, the trouble and
  annoy !

503

" But *You*, who, when with him you lived, received from
  him of old,
Rare honours, glory, fame, sweet boons and graces manifold,
O is it right against him now your bosom you should
  steel,
And leave him lonely all and sad, affliction's scourge to
  feel ?

504

"O Lady mine! do virtuous deeds, sweet actions good
    and kind,
Enjoy a happy, prosperous life, [and with a tranquil
    mind,]
And live in love, as wills the heart, unto that lordly
    King,
So far renowned." Thus to a close the dame her speech
    did bring.

505

These words the Lady heard : At once she was inflamed
    with ire,
As if her bosom were burnt up with wrath's consuming
    fire.
Forth from her seat she started up, in anger and amaze :
Then at her did her serving-dame, the Crooked Lady,
    gaze.

506

The Queen she seized, and by the neck, and pulled her
    by the same,
And thrust her straight within the room, and then the
    Crooked Dame
Tugged at the rope with violence, the rope upon the door,
And stood outside the chamber straight [with turmoil
    and uproar.] *

507

The Queen marked how the aged Dame was standing,
    there and then,
Like fire her anger hotter grew, and hotter grew again !
Like to a female cobra she, all passionately enraged,
With harsh and hard expressions thus the fierce conten-
    tion waged :

          * See Notes.

508

" You who have spoken shameless words, deceitful words
and lies,
Now I shall beat until I make your hunchback less in
size !
Your tongue will I pull out, and lay your shameless
boasting low,
And like the dust will scatter it, and make it far to go ! "

509

Now while the Queen was wrangling thus, the fearless
Crooked Dame
Tugged at the door, and shrilled aloud the great and
lustrous fame,
The mighty glory, far-renowned, of KUSA, King and
Lord,
Thus did the ancient Dame recount, with many a search-
ing word :

510

"O is there any King on earth of equal power and
might
With that all-glorious King, whose fame is ever clear
and bright ?
Or one who has such radiant town, one prosperous without bound,
As is the city of the gods [that in the heavens is found] ?

511

" His full array of infantry, cars, elephants, and steeds,
His waiting servants, men and maids, his cattle of all
breeds,

His rich possessions, gems and pearls and precious jewels
    rare,
Are numberless! [With him, the KING, may never king
    compare!]

512

" To him, the Lord of all the world, that ever-radiant
    King,
Vast DAMBADIVA'S minor kings great store of presents
    bring ;
To him they offer priceless gifts, and bathe them in the
    rays
Of his resplendent feet, which shine with undiminished
    blaze!

513

" His voice, like fearless lions' roar, in all directions goes,
And falls upon the ears of kings, the hostile kings, his
    foes ;
Upon their ears like iron-bars red-hot and keen it falls !
[And every listener, high or low, with terror it appals !]

514

"So gifted and renowned a King, through you, and you
    alone,
See how he bears keen misery, that rarely gifted One.
Your heart, if 'tis not softened now, [can be a heart no
    more,]
But hard and all-unfeeling 'tis, as mass of iron ore !

515

" O listen, therefore, to my words : Delay, delay no more,
Not even for a little while : but live with plenteous
    store

Of love and true affection hence unto your King and
    Lord :
[So will your after-lives be passed in honour and accord]."

516

When she, the Crooked One, had said these words, and
    not a few,
The Queenly Lady, passionately, all hot and wrathful
    grew;
And thus to daunt and frighten her, the ancient Crooked
    Dame,
In harsh, hot, angry words like these, then did the Queen
    exclaim :

517

" You vaunt, *There's no one but myself!* You grow so
    cool and bold,
No single loving word to me you tenderly have told.
If *I* come forth, if *I* come forth, I shall not fail to show
You have a mistress, Madam, yet ; and I can teach you
    so ! "

518

Now at the time the Crooked One these several phrases
    heard :
She struck and pulled the door with force : [she would
    not be deterred !]
And being bold and fearless too, and passionately
    wroth,
Thus did she speak : [old dames indeed to rail are seldom
    loth !]

519

" Those who possess rare beauty's dower grow arrogant
    and proud :
Though, ignorant of all the facts, with ire you cry
    aloud

Those bitter words, however wroth or angry you may
    seem,
I also know a shrewd device to match your present
    scheme.

520

"Now I will tell your Sire, the King, how, for your sake
    alone,
King KUSA famed has hither come and menial service
    done,
And worn him out with slavish toils: thus will I tell
    him all,
And portion not less wearisome on *you* will then befal!"

521

The Crooked Dame's harsh words severe, like molten
    metal fell
Upon the ears of her, the Queen, dismaying her right
    well;
Her heart with terror trembled sore, with mingled fear
    and shame:
And thus with sorrowing accents, she besought the
    ancient dame:

522

"O mother dear! who reared me well, in fitting mode and
    meet!
Whose kind, parental love increased, affection ever sweet!
Who gave me gifts I love to own, dear presents fair and
    gay,
Who, when I asked and sought a boon, did never say
    me nay!

523

" If he, the mighty King, our Sire, once learns the Lord
  is here,
King Kusa, on that very day, for me will fate severe
Straightway impend ; for cĕrtain as to earth your hand
  falls down,
If you strike at it, [so will he expel me from the town]."

524

She spoke unto the Crooked One : delicious words were
  they,
Bestowing comfort on the dame : and therewith took her
  way
Inside the royal Palace Hall, and therein did abide
In grief : [for further need was none of haughtiness or
  pride.]

525

When seven months, [long dreary months,] were flown,
  and vanished o'er,
And, all the while, our Bōdisat, with love and longing
  sore,
For Prabavati, in the town of Sāgala had stayed,
And grief intense and manifold had borne all unallayed :

526

Coarse food he ate, rough, wretched clothes, unseemly
  garb, he wore :
His time he spent in sleeplessness, [for sorrow vexed
  him sore.]
Then did his mind, [disturbed and tried by woe no man
  may speak,]
Become tormented by despair, and troubled much, and
  weak.

527

At last, our BŌDISAT removed the longing from his
heart,
And thought :—"Unto my Mother now, and Sire, will I
depart,
And see my parents once again, [and greet my native
shore,]
This Dame is no concern of mine ; here will I stay no
more ! "

END OF THE EIGHTH PART.

PART IX.

The Gathering of the Seben Kings:
Queen Prababati's Lament.

528

By virtue of King KUSA'S worth and high desert—the
Lord
Who practised ten high attributes, [required of One
adored,]
And who, as BUDDHA, afterwards brought heavenly joy
to men—
Through his desert, the rocky seat of SAKRA glowed
again.

529

Then SAKRA, with his thousand eyes, his thousand eyes
divine,
Looked forth upon the world of men [with countenance
benign],
And saw the Lordly One worn-out with weariness and
care,
At not obtaining his beloved, sweet PRABAVATI fair.

530

Then did the Lord of thousand eyes, cause letters to be
    writ,
As if by royal MADU sent, [with courtly phrase and fit,]
And sent to seven neighbouring Kings, o'er seven realms
    who reigned
[And in the missive each received this message was
    contained :]—

531

" Like to a goddess in the sky, my radiant daughter fair,
Sweet PRABAVATI beautiful, has left the halls and care
Of far-renowned King KUSA now, and hither has she
    come,
And makes within our city here abiding place and home.

532

" So, speedily come hither straight, and take her for your
    Bride—
My daughter, PRABAVATI fair, and home return with
    pride."
Thus were the letters written all—[each did the same
    contain,]
And to the seven Kings were sent, [each in his own
    domain.]

533

With joy then did the seven Kings renowned the letters
    view :
Each took a gallant fighting host, equipped in order
    due,
And forth they went, and on they sped, until they lighted
    down,
And pitched their camps upon the plain near SĀGALA's
    proud town.

534

When they beheld each other there, each sought from
    each to know
The motive that induced them all unto that spot to
    go.
And when for PRABAVATI famed—on her account
    alone—
They heard it was, right passionate the Kings grew every
    one !

535

With MADU they were wrothful all : [their ire was high
    and keen ;]
They said unto each other oft :—" [Was e'er such gather-
    ing seen ?]
For one, one only daughter—one, the daughter of the
    King,
We seven are summoned hither now : [it is a monstrous
    thing !"]

536

Then to the King a message curt they sent, a message
    keen,
And said :—"Give PRABAVATI now unto us as a Queen ;
Upon us seven bestow her straight ! If not, in full
    array,
Will we wage war [upon thy realm, and devastate and
    slay] ! "

537

King MADU heard the message told : and straight
    assembled then
A council of his ministers and honourable men :

                            K

And, point by point, the message he unto them all conveyed :
Then rose the courtly ministers—and this is what they
said :

538

" The seven haughty Monarchs here, with troops of
warriors bold,
O'er rampart walls and buttresses will leap and storm
the hold,
The city will they enter thus, as a destructive host—
[Our fair and ancient city, now so long our pride and
boast.]

539

" But ere our town and warriors all are ruined and destroyed,
[One course is yet before us, Sire, and that should be
employed :]
Thy daughter PRABAVATI, Queen endowed with beauty
rare,
Let her be taken to the foe, and from the city fare."

540

The King, their counsel hearing, [straight made thus
rejoinder free :]
" If unto *one* we give the Dame, the rest will angry be,
The other six ; and therefore now, [well be it understood,]
The course you would suggest to me is neither fit nor
good.

541

" Since she forsook the King supreme, great DAMBA-
DIVA'S Lord,
KUSA the great, and hither came, she will obtain reward ;

Yea, full reward and fivefold too, her deeds to her will
    bring,
Since she forsook the mighty lord, great DAMBADIVA's
    King!

542

" In seven parts will I divide her body, fresh and fair ;
To each of all the seven Kings will I despatch a share !
Thus will I from the town avert the woes that now
    impend ! "
So spoke the Monarch to his Court, [and from the Hal'
    did wend.]

543

Now what the Monarch had declared was speedily made
    known
By gossipry the Palace through, [so fast the news had
    flown ;]
And all the waiting men and maids, who did their
    service there,
The tidings heard with aching hearts, with sorrow and
    despair !

544

To PRABAVATI, bathed in tears, her seven sisters went ;
Saluting her, they held her close in fond embraces pent ;
They kissed her o'er and o'er again, their hearts opprest
    with fear ;
They spoke, and then away they went—[a goodly group
    and dear :]

545

Unto the Palace Chamber proud, where dwelt the stately
    Queen,
Their Mother, did they next proceed. Sore grieved in
    heart and mien

By fear of her impending death, the destiny severe,
Was PRABAVATI beautiful, [the Princess ever dear.]

546

As shake the tender leaves when forth the fleet gale
　　hurries o'er
[The forest lands], so did their hearts then shake and
　　tremble sore ;
And PRABAVATI, with the seven, her sisters passing fair,
Made sad lament with woeful words, in passionate
　　despair :

547

" Of gallant MADU I am child, the great and gracious
　　King :
O Mother ! from your womb I came, nor did I trouble
　　bring !
Reared with my sisters, hand in hand, sweet pastimes
　　have I known;
Now must I bid you all farewell, and journey forth
　　alone !

548

" My hair, my lustrous hair, that like the peacock's
　　feathers shone,
And gladdened eyes and hearts of those who loved to
　　look upon
Its jetty tresses beautiful, ere many days are fled,
Demons and fiends and ghouls will tear and rend, [when
　　I am dead.]

549

" My Mother ! when will you behold this narrow brow
　　of mine,
Delightful, that was wont, [you said,] like crescent moon
　　to shine

On PRABAVATI !—upon me ! . . . the narrow forehead
  fair,
Which ever gave beholders' hearts and eyes a pleasure
  rare ?

550

" Beside my ears, the tiny ears that shine like lotus
  bright
[And nestle deep], the loathsome birds, the carrion crow,
  will light,—
The crow and kite will there alight, and pluck these eyes
  of mine,
That cause the hearts of men to thrill with joy and bliss
  divine.

551

" The headsmen, in their horrid guise, with cunning
  cruel art,
Will cut my rounded breasts away [above my tender
  heart]—
The plump, full breasts, like golden swans, that cause to
  all that see
A joy ecstatic to arise, and fill their souls with glee.

552

" Upon the fingers of my hands, long, taper, rosy red,
And radiant as a blossomed flower, [that gentle dews have
  fed,]
Foul birds, with greed to gorge and feed, will light, and
  seize, and fly,
And bear them [far from home and you], unto the
  wombèd sky.

553

"Vultures and kites in ravenous flights, instinct with
    cruel greed,
My poor remains will fatten on—[a cruel fate indeed];
The tips of their keen talons they will fix upon their
    prey,
And upwards fly into the sky, and bear the flesh away!

554

" Monsters and fiends in numerous throngs will come to
    feed on me,
The blood thick streaming from their mouths, right
    horrible to see!
My lovely limbs will they devour—the limbs that wont
    to be
In shapeliness like to the stem of gold banana-tree.

555

"So that I may be given away to seven Kings, who
    wage
War's deadly game, and seek in fight their armies to
    engage,
My shining hands, feet, throat, and trunk, and breasts,
    the snowy twain,
Must now with cruel craft be cut, and far asunder ta'en!

556

" This day, O whither will my waist, so dainty, have to
    go?
That weary road, that dreary road, I never now shall
    know;

The waist as slim as was the shaft of KĀMA's famous
  bow,
Bewitching all who looked at it, [delighting high and
  low ! "]

557

Thus speaking words of woe, of woe, the daughter of the
  King,
Fair PRABAVATI, sobbed amain, and wept, and down did
  fling
Her at her Mother's feet, and claspt, and trembled sad
  and sore,
As shakes the graceful, golden vine, [when winds are
  thundering o'er.]

END OF THE NINTH PART.

PART X.

The Reconciliation.

558

By royal MADU'S high command, the Torturer came along;
Like to a dreadful monster he, huge, terrible, and strong!
In red apparel was he dight, [a hideous, bloody red;]
And clustering flowers of scarlet-bloom his body garlanded.

559

A ruddy man with saffron smeared; within his hand he swung,
And brandished oft, a massy club [hard, knotty, stout and long];
Of palm-flower juice * a bellyful he swallowed greedily,
Whereby vexatious words and fierce and savage forth growled he!

560

His bloodshot eyes he whirled around; an axe and block he brought,
A block for chopping flesh upon! Revolting to the thought,

* See Notes.

And of a figure terrible, he speedily came nigh :
And while he thus approached the Tower, the royal
 Palace high,

561

As shake the leaves when rapid winds assail them on
 the bough,
So PRABAVATI in her heart was sorely trembling now :
She shook, she trembled ; for the fear of death assailed
 her sore,
That Queenly Dame, that Queenly Dame [had courage
 now no more].

562

The Queen, her Mother, seeing all, and grieving in her
 soul,
Without or stop or stay went forth—[can mothers e'er
 control
Their love ?]—went forth unto the King, and at his feet
 fell down,
King MADU's feet, and thus [her woes, her woes and
 wish] made known :—

563

"Oh ! is it true, O Sire and Lord, your daughter and
 mine own,
The lady PRABAVATI, now, [the daughter of the throne,]
Shall be in portions parcelled out, and cut in pieces seven,
And to the Kings [beyond the walls, the warring Kings]
 be given ?"

564

Unto the Queen, who question asked, the King made
 answer free :
"Unto the Kings, the seven Kings, who seek to wage
 with me

A war, a cruel, bloody war, and hither armies bring,"
[Thus spoke unto his grieving spouse that wise and wily
    King]—

565

" Unless to them, and each of them, I give a share of
    her,
In seven portions parcelled out, with just division fair,
Exactly cut, [unless this course I take, my stately
    Queen,]
To pacify the seven Kings will be a trouble keen !

566

" Since she of high King KUSA said—*His beauty is but
    small,*
Forsook him next, and made her looks pre-eminent over
    all
Other things, and hither came, the meed she shall
    obtain
Shall far abroad through all the world be now made
    clear and plain !

567

" Her body cutting into seven, in seven portions true,
And well divided, now will I—this is what I shall do—
Give to the Kings " (thus spoke the King), " and satisfy
    them all :
And save my city and my realm, [and keep them free
    from thrall."]

568

The Queen was sad and sore distrest, for woe had
    entered in ;
She heard the utterance of the King, [nor grace from
    him could win.]

To PRABAVATI going then, she wept, she wept amain,
And thus with lamentations sore the Queen to speak
was fain :

569

" By your sad plight and you, mine Own, we see, we see
with speed
The ill that mortal folk befals who counsel will not
heed,
Nor listen to the words of those, the well disposed and
kind :
That ill and sore calamity here instanced well we
find.

570

"[King OKĀVAS] displayed his might, and with his
wreath-like fame
He graced the earth as gauds adorn the shoulders of a
dame;
On heads of DAMBADIVA's kings, upon each Rajah's head,
He set his feet, which are as flowers, and far his glory
spread :

571

"To him, King OKĀVAS renowned, lord of the Solar line,
Who well resembled sunbeams bright, that ever gaily
shine
And glad the water-lily plots, the lily-garden rare,
That famous King who held the town of KUSĀVATI
fair :

572

" In virtues well was he bestead, and, like the *Wishing
Tree*,
Rare gifts and generous he bestowed, a noble King was
he,

Of lofty rank and lineage high, [a lineage none may
    scorn :]
To him, that Monarch far renowned, unto that King was
    born

573

"A goodly Prince, of high desert and famed, in sixty-
    four *
High sciences well versed and skilled, with voice like
    lion's roar,
Prince KUSA, whose distinguished fame was far and
    widely known,
Through all the wide world's vast extent had it with
    splendour flown.

574

"Yet *You*, too proud of your good looks, too proud and
    arrogant,
Forsook him straight, because, forsooth, his beauty was
    but scant,
And by our speeches set no store, but hither madly
    came :
Meet retribution do you win indeed, a meed of fame !

575

"O if a son you had brought forth, a glory-laden
    boy,
That Monarch's son [and heir of all his parents might
    enjoy],
Would not the Kings of all the earth great love to you
    have shown,
And high affectionate regard to you, to you alone?

* See Notes.

576

"Those seven Kings, those haughty Kings, who vauntings
not a few
Have proudly said, and hither come but for the sake of
you,
To take you from your home away, and strong array
have led
Of seven armies well equipt, [war's deadly path to
tread ;]

577

" If he, the great and ·goodly King, King KUSA of
renown,
This very moment now abode in this our royal town,
[Then would those Kings] rush wildly forth [at sight of
him, the bold],
As lions blind, or elephants all hot and uncontrolled.

578

" But now,—since you forsook that King, the King of
lofty state,
Possessed of such rare might, and power, and strength—
the truly great,
Disdainfully abandoned him, and to this town withdrew,
Alas! a bitter, cruel death befals this day to you !"

579

With such like words the weeping Queen, with sorrow
troubled sore,
King KUSA's rare magnificence recounted o'er and o'er :
As if it were ineffable magnificence—[I ween]
King KUSA's fame was nobly told by her, the weeping
Queen !

580

But PRABAVATI hearing it, said :—" KUSA here *doth*
    dwell ;
For me, on my account alone, [because he loved me
    well,]
He hither came, and here abides within this very place,
King KUSA, stately lord, and head of the great Solar
    Race."

581

The Lady Mother, when she heard the speech, thus
    answering cried :
" O PRABAVATI ! say you so, because death's at your
    side ?
O do you speak deliriously since death is coming nigh —
And coming very speedily ?" Thus did the Mother cry.

582

When PRABAVATI heard these words, they hindered her
    no more :
" Look out ! " (she said,) " and see the chief of DAMBA-
    DIVA'S shore !
King KUSA, far renowned, is there ! So drive your doubts
    away ;
For him assuredly you see ! " Thus did the Lady say.

583

Thus did she speak, and called the Queen, and climbing
    up the stair,
Unto an upper chamber both did thereupon repair.
And by her daughter to the Queen were fully told and
    shown
The marks and features all whereby King KUSA might
    be known.

584

Now, when she said :—" The menial there who washes
down below

Those greasy pitchers, and with soot and filth is covered
so,

Like to a cook, a grimy cook, is he the Lordly King,

The monarch KUSA [far renowned, whose praise all
nations sing] !"

585

Forth burst the Lady, hearing it, in anger hot and high,

And with her daughter much enraged, did thus in passion cry :—

" Are *you* an outcaste damsel now, or girl of low degree ?

Or maiden of plebeian birth? [I pray you, answer
me !"]

586

The Lady Mother thus exclaimed : and PRABAVATI
fair,

Endowed with beauty excellent, all dainty, sweet and
rare,

Told what she knew with pleasing words ambrosially
sweet,

[And thus replied unto the Queen in courteous wise and
meet :]

587

" No outcaste maid am I, [she said,] or born of humble
line !

King KUSA's high magnificence and state [which once
were mine]

I know right well and thoroughly ; and all the brilliant
sheen

Of his prosperity and power have I both shared and
seen !

588

Now every day and all, within that Monarch's Palace
tall,

Do twenty thousand Brahmans come and throng the
lordly Hall   ∾

(Right well they know the Vedas* four), and there with
food are served,

Meet sustenance and savoury food, [ne'er from the
board *they* swerved !]

589

" [Of elephants] that touch the earth with seven stout
limbs of might,

Who crush and conquer enemies right in the thick of
fight,

Of these, full twenty thousand beasts, high-spirited and
strong,·

Right goodly beasts, in proud array, crowd all the streets
along.

590

" And troops of horses numberless, that touch the earth
with five

[Extremities, as noble steeds as man may seek to
drive],

In colour like the prancing waves upon the Milky
Main,

Abound within the lordly town, and throng each street
and lane !

591

" And twenty thousand chariots fair are there within
the town,

With charioteers all gallantly careering up and down !

* See Notes.

The spiry pinnacles atop of beaten gold are gay,
And golden banners on the tents in glorious shimmers
play !

592

" And beeves and oxen there are seen in numberless
array,
With golden rings upon their horns, all bright and
golden gay,
And tinkling ornaments besides [that peal a fairy
sound] ;
While drums and tomtoms on their backs are well-
secured and bound.

593

" From day to day, and every day, unto that Palace
Hall
Go twenty thousand damsels fair, right lovely are they
all,
With cows ; and gold and silver pails they carry to and
fro :
[In sooth, it is a noble sight—a rare and glorious show !]

594

" As when from earth you take a clod, the earth will
lessen none :
So, if all DAMBADIVA'S wealth were ta'en from his
alone,
That King's, it would diminish none ; for boundless is
it ever :
[Such are the wealth and majesty that wait on his
endeavour ! "]

L

595

With such delicious words did she, the stately lady
   fair,
Sweet PRABAVATI, praise the might and majesty so
   rare
Of high King KUSA to the Queen, her stately Mother
   there !
[Nor did she glowing eulogy upon his glory spare.]

596

Then was the dear delightful Queen made glad as is the
   Main,
The Milky Sea, when on it falls the moonlight's stream-
   ing rain !
She quickly went without delay unto the King, her
   lord,
And told each circumstance to him, each several phrase
   and word.

597

The Monarch heard : and next beheld the mighty,
   Lordly One :
Then entered fear, and fixed itself within his bosom's
   throne :
With courteous, pleasing words he spoke : [and thus this
   speech addressed
Unto King KUSA standing there, his son-in-law and
   guest :]

598

"O You, who set your flower-like feet upon the heads of
   Kings,
The Kings of DAMBADIVA'S realms ! who own a voice
   that rings

As loud and resonaut as is the king of lions' roar!
Resembling SAKRA: [Chief and Lord of DAMBADIVA's
    shore!]

599

"O Sire and Lord right excellent! I never was aware
You left your high, imperial state, and hither did
    repair;
And, doing service as a cook, [in menial guise and port,]
Within this royal town of ours abode and made re-
    sort.

600

"O Sire! if like the lotus leaf [that lets the drops
    depart],
The faults we did in ignorance You do not take to
    heart,
If, with not small indulgence now, our errors You for-
    give,
It will be high and gracious boon [to value while we
    live]!"

601

The Lordly One, on hearing it, thought:—"Harsh words
    if I speak,
Fear falling on him sore, perchance his very heart will
    break—
May break, and he will quickly die; and therefore I to-
    day
Shall seek to cheer and solace him, and words delicious
    say!"

602

Thus did he reason while he stood among the pitchers
    there,
[Such bowl and dish as cooks may use, right homely
    kitchen-ware.]

Then pleasant words he straightway spake, and in the
following wise,
And in the elder Monarch's. heart caused plenteous joy
to rise :

603

" O lofty MADU, stately King! for PRABAVATI fair
I left my high imperial state and hither did repair,
And wrought hard service as a cook . . . all unbecom-
ing toil :
To win dear PRABAVATI'S love, thus did I slave and
moil.

604

" For that these toils I underwent, the blame is all with
me—
To me and to my hand alone; none other may there be
To blame therefor—'twas *I* alone ! And hence, 'tis right
and fair
That I the consequences all alone should meet and
bear."

605

Now at this speech King MADU felt great joy within his
mind—
The speech the Lordly One had made, [so lovingly
inclined.]
Then went the elder Monarch forth—he went not slow
at all—
Forthwith unto the Royal Tower, the stately Palace
Hall.

606

Fair PRABAVATI then he called, and shrewdly to her
said,
With many a wise, sagacious word : " O now be quickly
sped

To KUSA, King renowned; and there, meet salutations
  done,
Forgiveness win and straight return!" Thus spoke the
  Kingly One.

607

She heard her royal father's words: her younger sisters
  she,
With all the ladies of her train, a joyous sight to see,
Took straightway forth, and soft attire adorningly put
  on,
Apparelled as a goddess is! [and sought the Lordly One.]

608

King KUSA, when he saw afar that peerless, queenly
  Dame,
As, like a royal female swan, she proudly to him came,
Thought thus:—" That lady's spirit high will I this in-
  stant prove:
[And bring repentance to her heart—a heart I dearly
  love!"]

609

With water from a pitcher he the ground well sprinkled
  o'er
A space in compass and extent like to a threshing-floor;
Of mud and glaur no little store, no little store was
  there;
The BŌDISAT stood in the midst—[he stood with
  haughty air].

610

Like as when, at a kalpa's end, fell down a golden vine
Struck by a strong, tempestuous gale, so fell that Dame
  benign;

But in she went, and through the midst ploughed she her
    onward road,
And rose, while ever in her heart increasing ardour
    glowed.

611

Then PRABAVATI laid her hands, her soft and tender
    hands,
Upon his feet, the Lordly One's, [the while he proudly
    stands :]
'Twas like a rosy lotus set upon a flower of gold,
A flower of thick and beaten gold !   And thus her wish
    she told :

612

" O Lordly One, all-glorious One ! who for my sake alone
Came to this town ! the great distress and sorrow you
    have known
And borne, while here, can ne'er be told ; nor ever can
    be said
The measure of the sore distress [inflicted on your head].

613

" Nor was *I* free from grief: thenceforth nor sleep nor
    slumber more
Came to mine eyes ; apparel foul, apparel vile I wore,
And savoury food I tasted none, no little sorrow bore,
And bore it all the while—in truth 'twas sorrow keen
    and sore !

614

"O Lordly One, all-glorious One ! if any fault be mine
That I have done, and if your grace and clemency be-
    nign

Increase, and you forgive the fault, and kindly pass it
o'er,
Then will the glory of your fame wax ever more and
more.

615

" But if with me you wrathful grow, upon that very tide,
The King, my Father, into seven just parcels will divide
My hapless frame, and take it hence, and have it straight-
way given
Unto the Kings belligerent, the hostile royal seven.

616

"So, Mighty Lord ! to you, to you is given, this very
day
The riches of my life to save, nor let them bear away
My body now, nor let me die ! O destiny severe !
O generous, lordly, lofty King, thy wife's entreaty hear !"

617

Thus when fair PRABAVATI spake, and all her sorrows
told,
And wept and sobbed lamenting sore, [all piteous to
behold,]
He, who in all these woes and griefs was yet to inter-
vene,
The BŌDISAT, majestic stood, and heard, [and mused
serene :]

618

" *Great Kings of old, with virtue graced, nor took to heart nor
chid*
The faults that poor benighted folks or little children did ;
And women's faults and poets' faults [were never visited
With punishment severe at all, but gently checked and chid].

619

"If angry with the Dame I grow, and wrathful words I
    speak,
Her soft and tender heart perchance with very woe will
    break,
And she will die, and what will then my sufferings all
    avail,
The labours I have undergone ?   [All, all my plans will
    fail!"]

620

Thus did he muse, and that he might all prosperous still
    remain,
And pass with her, his lovely Bride, a long and happy
    reign,
He straight consoled the peerless Queen, and spoke, and
    in this wise—
Thus did the Bōdisat [renowned, whose name we
    idolise]:

621

" O Prabavati, dearest Dame ! until my life is done,
No harsh, unkind, unpleasing act or deed, no single one,
By body, word, or mind* shall I, [my sweet and graceful
    Bride,]
Shall I do ever—never once, whatever may betide !

622

"So, fears dispelled, return, return unto your Palace
    Hall,
And eat, and drink, and merry make, and deck yourself
    withal

* See Notes.

In gay attire, and pass your life all meetly as you
    may."
[Thus spoke he to the stately Dame,] and sent her
    straight away.

END OF THE TENTH PART.

PART XI.

---◇---

The Bloodless Victory.

623

Now at that time, the Lordly King, of wisdom, skill, and
    pride,
King KUSA, that abroad he might the foemen scatter
    wide,
The enemies that girt the town, with strength and force
    afar,
Disperse them all, thus musing thought, [preparing him
    for war :]

624

" I, with a serried host, will go, and leap from spot to
    spot
Among the men, and show abroad the prowess I have
    got ;
And in the midst shall shout aloud [and all their senses
    stun],
With cries like to a lion's roar, that fearful is of none !

625

" When I to battle boune me forth, the hostile troops
    will flee,
Bewildered and amazed and stunned even at the sight of
    me !

And home again will I return, and bring the Kings renowned,
The seven hostile Kings, with me, their hands behind
them bound."

626

Thus did he muse, that stately King, all valorous and
wise,
While gladness in his heart arose [and beamed from
forth his eyes].
Glad was he as the lordly king of lions, bold and
stout,
When he among a troop of steeds with mettle sallies out.

627

Now as the Goodly One thus made the townsmen passing
fain
And glad, with words ambrosial sweet as is the Milky
Main,
Delicious words and rarely sweet ; and beamed on her
sweet heart
[Fair PRABAVATI'S], as the moonbeams high in heaven
apart!

628

That very day King MADU sent, with speed that very
day;
For love and high regard within waxed more and more
alway,
High wedding messengers he sent, [rare presents offer-
ing]
To him, King KUSA [far renowned, the brave and stately
King].

629

King Kusa shaved his downy beard, and bathed in water
    clear
And cool and scented [sweetly, too, with fragrance rare
    and dear] ;
And ornaments and soft attire he donned that very day,
That he more beautiful might seem, illustriously gay !

630

Abroad he gazed, and caused the earth to tremble at
    that tide,
His lustrous glory and renown proclaiming far and wide ;
That fame immeasurably great, that had no stay or
    bound,
Did he with wondrous deeds make known to all the
    world around !

631

He clapped his hands and clamour made ; he raised a
    roaring shout,
Like to a fearless lion's roar ; and, as he sallied out,
Attended by the ministers, so glorious did he shine,
He was in majesty as brave as monarchs all divine !

632

He mounted then an elephant—a beast by MADU sent,
And graithed with face-cloth many hued, and many an
    ornament,
With fan and nets and golden bells on ear and tusk
    and throat,
And golden coverlets* he bore—a gladsome beast, I wot !

* See Notes.

633

With glory like as SAKRA'S was, when, to the Titans'
    War,
Attended by a host of gods, he bound him forth afar,
Upon his beast Airāvana, so through the Eastern Gate
Sped KUSA then: and, close behind, fair PRABAVATI
    sate.

634

As when a hundred thousand peals of thunder shake the
    sky
[Upon a kalpa's close], and winds unceasing rage on
    high,
Such was his shout, as thrice he roared right loud, that
    all might hear:
" *Here I, King KUSA, world-renowned, among your hosts*
    appear! "

635

As flees thick darkness when at dawn the sun's bright
    beams appear;
As herds of elephants rush off when lion's roar they
    hear;
As bees that, seeing flame and smoke, fly fast and far
    away;
So straight into the jungle rushed the foemen's proud
    array!

636

Thus then the sun-descended* King stood on the battle-
    plain,
A glorious victor, far renowned, with seven monarchs
    ta'en,

* See Notes.

And bound in their own royal robes—the army of the
    foe
Chased to the woods!   Thus did he stand, and potent
    glory show !

637

With joy did SAKRA then behold the grand achievement
    done;
How, but with one loud lion-roar, the conquest he had
    won,
And captured seven Kings ; nor shed of blood so much
    as one
Small fly would drink, and, weaponless, had flung not
    e'en a stone !

638

Great SAKRA, lauding much, with joy sped to his
    heaven and throne :
But ere he soared, an eight-curved gem,* a priceless,
    lordly one,
Bright as the sun at morn, by him on KUSA'S neck was
    thrown :
And all famed KUSA'S ugliness for ever more was flown!

639

By virtue of that peerless gem, that on his neck was
    hung,
The BŌDISAT grew beautiful, as one the gods among,
Descended from the heavens to earth ! His past de-
    merits done,
Were cleared away, and all his hopes accomplished,
    every one!

* See Notes.

640

Then KUSA on the beast returned, beside his glorious
 Bride,
Unto the town with royal power, magnificence, and
 pride ;
Like SAKRA when, triumphantly, the Titans he had
 fought,
And back to heaven, with train of gods, fair SUJÁTÁVA
 brought !

641

With moon-like, star-like, wreath-like fame, with fame
 . like Kailas' Hill,
The Victor KUSA, strong of heart, did all directions
 fill !
The seven captive hostile Kings, their hands behind
 them tied,
Upon King MADU he bestowed right speedily ; and
 cried :

END OF THE ELEVENTH PART.

PART XII

The Bridal of The Seven Kings.

642

"O lordly King and glorious! the seven Kings are here,
The hostile Kings who threatened war, [and sought to cause you fear :]
Here are they all at your command: them, if you choose to slay,
Or grant their lives in charity, and let them go away:

643

"According to your wish and will unto them be it done :
[These captive monarchs hither brought—here are they every one."]
Thus to King MADU did he speak. That King heard all he said,
And thus the latter Lord at once a meet rejoinder made:

644

"O Sire, all-glorious Lord and Chief! to all the Kings of might,
Of DAMBADIVA'S many realms, and unto these in sight,

These seven Kings, no grace may be but what from *You*
    shall flow

[For *You* are Emperor of all, and grace and boons
    bestow].

645

" Therefore, what you, a god on earth, like SAKRA the
    divine,

According unto what you will, the action will be mine :

Not swerving from it in the least, the action shall be
    done ! "

Thus spoke the King, with concord high [his speech, a
    royal one].

646

The mighty Lordly One renowned heard what the
    Monarch said :

[And thus he mused within his heart, ere he rejoinder
    made :]

" If now these seven captive Kings, these stately Kings
    are slain,

What fair advantage would accrue ? and what would be
    the gain ? "

647

Thus did he muse; and that it might thereafter long
    endure

As a renowned and goodly deed, an action just and
    pure,

With words ambrosially sweet, [such speech as mortals
    prize,]

Our BŌDISAT rejoinder made—he answered in this
    wise :

M

648

" Let PRABAVATI'S sisters seven, her younger sisters
    fair,
Resplendent as the goddesses, with beauty sweet and
    rare,
Be given in marriage to the Kings, all blithesome and
    serene,
That each may homeward take a bride, his chief and
    foremost Queen."

649

When thus the BŌDISAT had said, King MADU heard it
    all,
[And straightway loudly forth did he in meet rejoinder
    call :]
"Right true it is, O glorious Lord! You are our Sovereign
    King,
Of all [within these wide-spread realms, and chief of
    everything].

650

"Then, since it is so, whatsoe'er may be your royal
    will,
Why do you ask *us* now to act, [for *you* are Master
    still ?]
Let it be done, let it be done, exactly as you please ;
For all within the state are bound to bow to your
    decrees ! "

651

Thus spoke the King. The lofty King, high KUSA of
    renown,
Straight made the folks embellish all the fair and lordly
    town :

Like to the city of the gods, divinely proud and fair,
He caused it straight to be adorned—he decked it every-
    where.
652
The fair Princesses next he called, and summoned to his
    side :
He made them dress in white attire—[as suits a bonny
    Bride]—
In white attire and soft withal, with gauds and jewels
    rare,
So that in splendour they outvied the goddesses so fair.

653
Their lily hands he took, and placed within the hands of
    those,
The seven Kings—on lotus red (that blushes like the
    rose)
Of seven-budded bloom, as if seven other buds were laid—
And, each with each, a goodly group and gathering were
    made.
654
Thus held he marriage festival, [a rare and witching
    sight,]
And poured fair water [on their hands, the honoured
    bridal rite].
And goodly maidens made he stand arrayed on either
    side,
Who "𝕸𝖆𝖞 𝖄𝖔𝖚𝖗 𝕷𝖎𝖛𝖊𝖘 𝖇𝖊 𝕷𝖔𝖓𝖌 𝕻𝖗𝖊𝖘𝖊𝖗𝖛𝖊𝖉 ! " with ac-
    clamations cried.*
655
Attended with their retinues, with glory meet and due,
With splendour and rare dignity, and presents not a few,

* See Notes.

The fair Princesses—seven they were—with loving words then bade
Farewell to all they left behind, and preparations made

656

To bear them to their several homes. The Lordly One bestowed
Upon the seven mighty Kings his leave to take the road,
Intrusting unto each his Bride, and forth he bade them fare,
Each to his stately town and realm—[a joyous host they were].

657

Then did the seven lordly Kings, ere they departure took,
Bathe in the radiance of his feet, that shone as shines a brook—
The feet of him, the Lordly One. Extinguishing the flame
Of fear, they severally went forth, [each Monarch with his Dame.]

658

Like to the sun in power and might, all glorious to behold:
Like Mēru's Mount in moveless strength [a staunch and massy hold]:
Like BRAHASPATI,* [he who taught the gods,] in rarest skill:
Like SAKRA in majestic weal, the first and foremost still:

* See Notes.

659

The Bōdisat right excellent, the very mighty One,
Took leave of his delighted Sire, since home he would be
    gone :
With loving words farewell he said, and with a proud
    array,
A gallant army well-equipped, he took his homeward
    way.

660

Then forth from Sāgala he fared, that sovereign Lord
    serene,
And took with him his royal spouse, the first and fore-
    most Queen,
The beauteous dame so fair to see, who like a goddess
    shone :
[There never was through all the world a more enchanting
    one !]

661

Forth fared they then upon the road, upon a glorious car,
Drawn by a white and prancing steed,* [that galloped
    fleet and far ;]
Upon the roof the golden flags, the streamers unconfined,
Shook still and danced right merrily as on them breathed
    the wind !

662

The hundred yoduns soon they passed. They halted
    here and there,
At halting-places on the road, the people's thoughtful care
(The people of both realms) had built [and decked and
    set apart
Where they, the royal Twain, might rest—might rest
    with joyous heart].

* See Notes.

663

As glads the lily-buds the Moon, the bright full Moon so
   fair,
And makes their blossoms all unclose, so did the royal
   Pair
Delight the hearts of all the folks.   And thus with regal
   state
They reached proud KUSĀVATI'S town, [and galloped
   through the Gate.]

END OF THE TWELFTH PART.

PART XIII.

—◇—

"And They Both Lived Happy Ever Afterwards!"

664

As doth the bright pea-hen* rejoice to hear the sound of
    rain,
[When thick and fast the heavy drops come pattering
    down amain,]
So did the high Queen Mother joy when [with a mur-
    murous hum]
The cry arose and spread abroad—*The Lordly One is come !*

665

With joy she went to meet the Twain, their dear ap-
    proach to greet,
And plenteous store of food she took, delicious food and
    sweet,
Of various sorts; and, followed by a fair and brave
    array,
A gallant army well equipped, to meet them by the way.

666

[They came ! They came ! The banners flapped, the
    trumpets sounded clear !]
But at that tide the BŌDISAT, and she, his Consort dear,

* See Notes.

Fair PRABAVATI, bent them low beside the royal
    feet
Of her, the high Queen Mother there, and did her rever-
    ence meet.

667

With pearly tears within her eyes the Queen bathed
    both the Twain,
And lovingly embraced them both, and clasped them
    close again !
Then did they all great solace find, and joy, and rare
    content
In presence of each other there : [and homeward thus
    they went.]

668

Like to great SAKRA, King of heaven, when he trium-
    phant came
From fields where he the Titans quelled [and brought
    them all to shame],
When, with the armies of two worlds attendant at his
    side,
He entered the fair town of heaven, the town of peerless
    pride!

669

Such was the Lordly One, at last all beauteous to
    behold !
And, while through all the city there, in festal state he
    rolled,
Delightful women came to look, as gloriously he went,
And gazed [and, as they gazed, their hearts were filled
    with rare content] !

670

The lovely damsels of the town arrayed them passing
    fair :
Their teeth with flowers of coco-palms might aptly all
    compare :
Their bosoms were like pitchers round, well-shaped of
    burnished gold :
[Such were they all within the town, bewitching to be-
    hold !]

671

And one—a lovely dame she was—who longed to see
    the King,
All hurriedly upon her neck her jewelled zone did
    fling ;
And [what should grace her shining throat—such was
    her heedless haste],
Her necklace, all of pearls bestrung, she put around her
    waist !

672

And as the women on the paths, on either side the
    way,
Stood grouped [in fascinating throngs, one then might
    aptly say],
The lustre from their eyes that shone was like long cords
    of blue,
To noose their youthful lovers' hearts and hold them
    ever true !

673

And royal dames within the town who still before that
    day,
Abode in lofty upper rooms, and never thence did stray,

Who ne'er had seen or sun or moon, upon that day were
    gone
Right in the middle of the street, and gazing stood, each
    one !

674

The dames and damsels of the town who longed to see
    the Lord,
The Lofty One, so well-beloved, were rapt with one
    accord :
Their eyelids down were never dropt : like goddesses on
    high
With glory's flame did they appear--[like tenants of the
    sky] !

675

And on that day, a woman there, who longed to see the
    King,
Had much delayed [for such there be deferring every-
    thing] :
At last she came, and ran with haste; while one hand
    fingered there
In putting on her gay attire, the other bound her hair !

676

Our Bōdisat all gloriously went to his Palace Hall :
His presence on his thronging folks made joy abundant
    fall,
As falls the Moon's soft paly beams [like streams of
    silver rain],
And gladden gaily as they fall, the placid Milky Main !

677

Obedient to the Queen's commands, the good Queen
  Mother there,
Our BŌDISAT delight enjoyed, distinguished bliss and
  rare !
Nor did he abrogate the rules and usages of yore,
Upheld by royal Kings of old, who swayed the realm
  before.*

678

With PRABAVATI, glorious Dame, the source of rare
  content,
His Queen, with rarest beauty graced, a happy life he
  spent.
Their days they passed as if twain lives in one were
  fully blent !
At last, unto the Town of Gods, through fair desert thᵉ
  went !

END OF THE LEGEND.

* See Notes.

679

When thus the Great All-Seer did the tale of KUSA
tell,
He made the hearts of gods and men with rare delight
to swell,
The eight Brahmanic strains sublime * to bruit abroad
he sought,
And of the Faith the four great truths he nobly preached
and taught.

680

The Priest who wearied of the rites, all for a woman's
love,
With twice five hundred Nāgas too, to higher grades did
move
Upwards and onwards, until they the *Sovan** stage
attained,
And high NIRVĀNA's perfect bliss eventually obtained.

681

He who was King and KUSA's sire, within that former
birth,
Is royal SUDDHODENA now ;* the dame of rarest worth,
Queen SĪLAVATI, greatly-famed, is MĀYA called by
name—
Great BUDDHA's Mother [far-renowned, in sooth, of
peerless fame].

* See Notes.

682

Prince JAYANPATI beautiful, is ANANDA the Priest,
[A holy man of high repute through all this golden
  East :]
The shrewd and gentle-hearted dame, who crooked was
  and low
Of stature, her at present as KUDUTTARA we know.

683

The royal throngs, that gathered round the stately
  Palace Hall,
Surround the great Chief Teacher now, his loved com-
  panions all !
The lady PRABAVATI now is YASŌDARA fair,
The mother she of RAHULA, [esteemed beyond compare.]

684

And he who by his mighty strength the royal power
  destroyed
Of seven Kings, seven hostile Kings, and made their
  efforts void,
King KUSA, far-renowned and great, the Lord of high
  degree,
Is chief and highest Buddha now . . . and, brethren,
  I am He !

The Author's L'Envoi.

685

There was a goodly Pandit, one who in Hisveligame
Abode, a greatly honoured man : DANDAJA was his
name.
Beyond the Triple Doctrine's Sea he reached the farther
shore,
By means of Wisdom's stately ship, that bore him safely
o'er !

686

And ALAGIYAVANNA [wise, who was that Pandit's
son],
A Household Secretary he, a virtue-seeking one,
So that he might NIRVĀNA win, this legend did rehearse—
THE LEGEND OF KING KUSA famed, in sweet delightful
verse.

687

When fifteen hundred years had passed, and thirty-two
beside,
From great King SAKA's * time—in May, and at the full
moon's tide,
At MENIKHĀMI's high request, the dame as goddess
fair,
The Poet-Secretary, sought by other poets rare,
Thus for the sake of endless bliss, devised in Sinhalese,
The KUSA LEGEND here made known !—[May his
endeavours please] !

* See Notes.

NOTES.

NOTE

NOTES.

FIRST PART.

1, 2, 3. THE ASCRIPTION OF WORSHIP.—As in Buddhistic works generally, the poem begins by ascribing honour and worship to the Founder of the Faith (BUDDHA), to the Doctrine (DHARMA), and to the Priesthood (SANGHA)—" the Triple Gem," so called. This is an usage common to the literature of all countries where Buddhism prevails, in proof of which may be cited the document (quoted in SCHLAGINTWEIT's *Buddhism in Tibet*, p. 184) relative to the founding of a monastery in Ladâk. By some (see HODGSON's *Illustrations of the Literature and Religion of Buddhists*, p. 102) it is held SANGHA should be rendered, not *Priesthood*, but *Congregation of the Faithful*. Possibly the original meaning may have been the latter; but the signification now attached to the word, in Ceylon at least, is certainly *the Priesthood*.

Buddha, the Doctrine, and the Priesthood, are invoked in the TUN SARANA, or threefold protective formulary, often repeated by believers. It is also repeated on the occasion of young Buddhist priests commencing their noviciate (*Eastern Monachism*, p. 23). The formulary runs thus :—

BUDHAN SARANAN GACH'HAMI [1]
DHAMMAN SARANAN GACH'HAMI
SANGHAN SARANAN GACH'HAMI

I take refuge in Buddha :
I take refuge in the Faith :
I take refuge in the Priesthood.

A parrot now in the Malwatta Vihâra (monastery) at Kandy, has been taught to repeat the first line ; and often exhibits, nowise

N

loth, his proficiency to visitors, greatly to the delight of the young monks and other pupils.

As regards the allusion in the second line of the first stanza, it is believed that some lotus flowers burst into blossom through the influence of the moon's rays. The lotus, as the emblematic flower of India, is a theme of perpetual allusion in Oriental poetry and mystical literature. The well-known Tibetan phrase, "OM MANI PADMI HUM!" means, literally, "O THE JEWEL IN THE LOTUS!" —that jewel signifying BUDDHA.

Stanza 4, as invoking a junto of greater and minor deities, hardly accords with the strict tenets of Buddhism. It may be held, perhaps, to mark to what extent the national creed had in Ceylon, at the date of the poem, A.D. 1610, become degenerate, corrupt, and overgrown with other and debasing forms of religious belief. King RĀJASINHA I. apostatised from Buddhism, and persecuted its followers with great severity, extirpating the priests and destroying their books, A.D. 1586. (ALWIS's *Introduction to the Sidat Sangarāva*, p. 206.)

BRAHMA, the creator of the universe, one of the Hindu Triad, consisting of him, of VISHNU, the Preserver, and SIVĀ, the Destroyer : all of whom are invoked in this stanza. BRAHMA is generally represented riding on a swan, and having four faces and four (not seven, as in the text) hands, emblematic of the four Vedas.

VISHNU, the Preserver, is the most popular deity of the Hindu Pantheon : and, according to PERCIVAL, commands, in his various manifestations, the worship of most of the inhabitants of India. He has had nine avatars; and in the tenth, he is to descend, mounted on a white horse, to the world again as a Reformer, punish the impenitent, bring back the Golden Age, and restore true religion. There is a temple dedicated to his worship at Kandy, and called, by way of distinction, the Maha (or Great) Dēwāla. The offerings to VISHNU consist of fruit, flowers, honey, incense, money, food, and the like. (*Land of the Vedas.*)

GANESHA, the god of wisdom and policy, is painted as a short, fat man, with a large paunch and the head of an elephant, sitting on a lotus and attended by a rat. To him invocations are made when any undertaking is begun, as when commencing a book, starting on a journey, or laying the foundation of a house.

SAKRA or INDRA, the Regent of the minor deities and Protector of beings in misery. See the notes appended to the 17th and 129th stanzas. *Swarga*, or the heaven occupied by this deity, is described as the most splendid the human mind can conceive. (PERCIVAL, p. 160.) Its palaces are composed of pure gold, resplendent diamonds, jasper, sapphire, emerald, and other precious stones, whose brilliance exceeds that of a thousand suns! Its streets are of crystal fringed with gold. The most beautiful and fragrant flowers adorn its forests, whose trees diffuse the sweetest odours. Refreshing breezes, canopies of fleecy clouds, thrones of dazzling brightness, birds of sweetest melodies, and songs of the most delightful harmony, are heard in the enchanting pleasances, which are ever fragrant, ever robed in summer green! This glowing description almost irresistibly reminds one, if it be not profane to institute the comparison, of BERNARD DE MORLEY'S noble hymn, *Jerusalem the Golden* :—

> "O one, O only mansion, O paradise of joy!
> Where tears are ever banished, where smiles have no alloy!
> With jaspers glow thy bulwarks, thy streets with emerald blaze,
> The sardonyx and topaz unite in thee their rays!
> Jerusalem the Golden, with milk and honey blest,
> Beneath thy contemplation sink heart and voice oppressed!
> The Prince is ever present, the light is aye serene,
> The pastures of the blessèd are decked in glorious sheen!"

ISWARA or SIVÁ, the Destroyer, the three-eyed god, is represented as presiding over reproduction and generation, as a symbol of which he rides on a white bull (*Land of the Vedas*, p. 203). According to Sir WILLIAM JONES, the worship of Sivá exhibits strong evidence of the connection between Hindu and Greek paganism. The most common symbol of Sivá is the *linga*, the phallus, which Professor WILSON considers the most ancient object of homage adopted in India subsequent to the ritual of the Vedas.

The remarkable inter-connection, so to speak, between Eastern and Grecian mythology, and the great likelihood of both of them, and the Norse mythology as well, having arisen from observations upon the ordinary phenomena of nature, and particularly of the movements of the sun, are well illustrated, and cogently reasoned upon in MAX MÜLLER'S most valuable and interesting essays, and in the introductory chapter of Cox's *Tales of the Gods and Heroes*. For a widely diverse hypothesis, however, every reader should consult—he is sure to do so with ample pleasure and profit—Mr GLADSTONE'S *Homer and the Homeric Age*.

THE GOD OF KATRAGAM is the favourite name among the inhabitants of Ceylon for KARTIKEYA, the son of Siva, the Mars of Eastern mythology. He is sometimes worshipped under the title of Mahasen, "the Lord of Great Armies." Mahasen, it may be added, was also the name of one of the most powerful kings of the island, the last of the Great Dynasty, who died A.D. 302, and was afterwards deified by his people.

The village of Katragama is in the south-east of Ceylon, and about thirty miles from the writer's present station, Hambantota. To the shrine at Katragama flock thousands of pilgrims every year from remote parts, not only of Ceylon, but of the continent of India, and even from remote Kashmir. The season of the year at which the pilgrimage occurs is nearly always a sickly one: and occasionally very sad scenes take place. A terrible outbreak occurred in this way in 1858, during which year the writer was stationed at Galle, in the Southern Province. The pilgrims were attacked by epidemic after epidemic, and perished in great numbers. Whether the diseases were brought by them to Katragama, or sprang into sudden life and energy there spontaneously—all the predisposing causes of unhealthy locality, exposure, unwholesome and scanty food, bodily weakness and weariness, and overstrung nervous excitement, being abundantly present—was disputed; but, once introduced, their ravages were appalling. Regardless of the rites they had travelled so far to take part in, regardless of the closest ties of kindred or friendship, the panic-stricken pilgrims fled for their lives, leaving, in many cases, their companions to perish by the waysides; and spreading the pestilence wherever they went. Like wildfire, cholera ran from hamlet to hamlet, from station to station. It was piteous to see forlorn women, forsaken by their husbands, their children dying beside them, wailing in all the agony, short-lived but almost incredibly passionate, of Oriental grief, and recalling forcibly the awful scene of bereavement recorded in Scripture—" In Rama was there a voice heard, lamentation and great mourning, Rachel weeping for her children, and would not be comforted, because they were not."

In view of so grievous a visitation, which is by no means rare, it is worthy of consideration whether restrictions may not wisely be imposed as to the yearly pilgrimages to Dewundra and Katragama, which attract thousands, and scatter, too often, disease broadcast through the country. Needless interference with religious prejudices cannot be sufficiently deprecated ; but at times interference is an imperative duty in the interests of the community at large.

Readers to whom the great Indian Epic, the *Rāmayana*, is familiar, may be interested in learning that the hamlet of Katragama is pointed out by tradition as the place at which the second nuptials of RĀMA and SITA were celebrated. Between twenty and thirty miles from Katragama, and a like distance from Hambantota, and off the south-east coast of Ceylon, are the Basses Rocks, which figure prominently in legendary story as being the last remnant of the stronghold of RĀVANA, whose abduction of SITA is the ground-work of the *Rāmayana*, the original, if it be not heresy to say so, of "the tale of Troy divine." The name of the rock among the inhabitants round about is still Rāvanankōtta, "the fortress of Rāvana," and it is not unusual to receive letters for the native crew on board the lightship at the rock, superscribed by that word, showing that the name is familiar in far-away places. How grand a stronghold it was, how long a siege, crowded with all the most terrific incidents of warfare, it underwent, and how eventually it, and the valiant band of Rakshas who defended it, fell before the united attack of RĀMA and his allies, is to be read in the *Rāmayana*, the oldest work, it may readily be assumed, in which Ceylon figures. It is quite possible the myth may have had some historic foundation. The singular absence of coral (which abounds else-where all round Ceylon) off the shore at Hambantota, and for many miles to the east and west of that station, is by some held to be evidence of submersion within a comparatively recent period. Many places in Ceylon bear appellations suggestive of episodes chronicled in the famous Epic.

As regards the Basses Rocks, the Rāvanankōtta of old, one may be tempted to say, looking at it from the bleak and barren shore between Kirinda and Yāla, *Fuit Ilium et ingens gloria*. But who can deny that a brighter and more abiding glory now attaches to the spot, in that, night after night, in still or stormy weather, there flashes from it a constant radiance, a friendly beacon-light of guid-ance and good cheer to voyagers on the high seas ?

THE SUN GOD.—PERCIVAL observes that the sun, both as a luminary and as personified under various titles, is a great object of Hindu worship. As in England, so in Hindustan and Ceylon, the first day of the week is named in honour of the sun. Royal families in the East pride themselves on being descended from the great Solar Dynasty, the *Suriyaransa*. In token of this, it may be noted, the entrance to the old palace at Kandy, now occupied by the chief Civil Officer residing at the station, is embellished with representations of the sun. So too the Written Rock at Kirinda near Hambautota. It will be seen in the course of the poem that King KUSA claimed descent from the Solar Line.

SURIYA, the sun god (says SOUTHEY, in a note to *The Curse of Kehama*, quoting Sir W. JONES), is believed to have descended frequently from his car in a human shape, and to have left descendants in various countries on earth, who are equally renowned in Indian story with the Heliadai of Greece.

THE SNAKE-GOD, Anantaya ("the infinite"), the ruler of the Nāga (snake) world, a being of supernatural powers, who is said to have listened to BUDDHA'S preaching with great reverence and devotion. The *nāga* or cobra is regarded by the Sinhalese with peculiar respect, and their legendary lore is full of allusions to it. Snake worship is one of the most ancient and wide-spread forms of religion in all parts of the world. It prevailed in Persia, in Greece, in Rome, among the Norsemen, the Mexicans, the wild tribes of Africa. Not improbably, the Druidic circles found in many parts of Britain are symbolical of it. As Colonel Forbes (*Eleven Years in Ceylon*) suggests, by *nāgas* we ought, in all likelihood, to understand *nāga*-worshippers, who were subsequently converted to the purer faith of Buddhism.

5. BHUWANEKA BĀHU VII., King of Ceylon, reigned at Kōtta, A.D. 1534–1542. He suppressed an insurrection in the earlier part of his reign. Meeting with much opposition, he placed his adopted son, afterwards King DHARMAPĀLA, under the protection of the Portuguese ; and sent an ambassador to Lisbon with a golden statue of the prince, to ask for aid. In 1540 the prince was christened in effigy at Lisbon by the name of DON JUAN, after DON JUAN of Austria: and an auxiliary force accompanied the ambassador on his return to Ceylon. The King was accidentally shot through the heart by a Portuguese gentleman on the Kelani river. (See TURNOUR'S *Epitome of Ceylon History*, prefixed to the Ceylon Calendar and Register for 1833.) The sending of the golden statue to Europe may have suggested one of the main incidents of this poem.

6. *Adigār* was the highest title given to an officer of state under

the Kandyan kings, and answered, perhaps, to Prime Minister or Generalissimo. The next highest was Disâva, or Governor of a province.

8. King RÂJASINHA ("Royal Lion") I. reigned A.D. 1581-1592. His was a stormy and eventful reign of eleven years, full of wars and contentions. As mentioned in a previous note, he forsook Buddhism, and, embracing Hinduism, distinguished himself by persecuting, with the usual fervour of an apostate, the followers of his early creed. A successor, however (WIMALA DHARMA, A.D. 1592-1604), was a devoted Buddhist, and zealous in re-establishing the national church. In his reign, the DALADA (the celebrated Tooth Relic, held in especial reverence by Buddhists in all parts of the world, as the most authentic relic of their Great Teacher) was removed to Kandy, where it now remains—the object of enthusiastic veneration on the part of three hundred millions of people ! It is frequently exhibited : the last two occasions on which the writer saw it being in December 1864, when it was shown to H.R.H. the DUKE OF BRABANT, the present King of the Belgians ; and again in July 1865, during the continuance of the great yearly festival, the Perahera, at Kandy. In the shrine containing the relic, which rests on a gold lotus inclosed within the innermost, also of pure gold, of seven caskets, is jewellery reputed to be of enormous value. The relic bears not the least resemblance whatever to a human tooth.

10. Powdered sandal-wood dissolved in water used by high-caste women to mark the part of the forehead between the eyebrows. The custom does not now prevail among the Sinhalese. In various parts of India, and among the Tamil races in Ceylon, it is customary to besmear this part of the forehead.

The following note is from *The Curse of Kehama* :—

" Hindoos, especially after bathing, paint their faces with ochre and sandal-wood, ground very fine into a pulp. The women occasionally wear a round spot, either of sandal, or of a preparation of vermilion between the eyebrows, and a stripe of the same running up the front of the head."

11. The Triple Gem—Buddha, the Faith, the Priesthood.

12. The plover is said by the Sinhalese to guard her eggs by

lying on her back over the nest and holding her feet upwards, fearing that the sky may fall and crush them !

The silvery whiteness of the yak's tail is well known. Of it was made the *chamāra*, the white fan or whisk, one of the five insignia of royalty. The remaining four are said to be the white umbrella or canopy, the sword, the crown or golden circlet for the forehead, and the golden sandals.

Colonel TORRENS thus describes (*Travels in Ladāk and Kashmir*, p. 124) the yak, which he first fell in with at Lahoul, where, by the way, Buddhism prevails :—" The yak is short, but of immense frame and strength, with-a small head, short horns, and long black hair reaching to the ground, beneath which is a sort of undergrowth of short, soft wool." According to VANDERHOEVEN (*Handbook of Zoology*, ii. p. 660) the yak (*bos grunniens*) occurs in Tibet both in the wild and tame state. It has long hair and a long-haired tail, like that of a horse.

The great precepts or obligations of Buddhism are ten in number, and are thence called *Dasa Sil*. The five first forbid—1. The Taking of Life. 2. Theft. 3. Adultery. 4. Lying. 5. The Use of Intoxicating Drinks.

These five should be repeated by true believers every day. In addition to the above, are five others which forbid—6. The eating of solid food after midday. 7. Attendance on dancing, singing, music, or plays. 8. The adornment of the body with flowers, and using perfumes and unguents. 9. Sitting on lofty or luxurious seats or couches ; and 10. Receiving gold or silver.

In deference to a simple process in what may be called practical mnemonics, the numbers five and ten were probably chosen by BUDDHA in order the more impressively to check off, finger by finger, the several rules when preaching to his hearers, who, in their turn, would by the same means readily recall them.

The eight first (called, as in the text, *A ta Sil*, the eight rites) should be repeated on *poya* days, the festival days at each change of the moon. All the ten obligations are at all times binding on the priests, who, as vowed to celibacy, construe the third to prohibit marriage (*Manual of Buddhism*, p. 483).

For priests advanced further in the religious life, more severe observances were laid down. To quote from MAX MÜLLER's *Buddhism, and Buddhist Pilgrims*, " They were not allowed to wear any dress, except rags collected in cemeteries, and a yellow robe (*siyura*) was to be thrown over them. Their food was to be extremely simple; and they were not to possess anything but what was received in alms collected from door to door in a begging-bowl. They had but one meal in the morning. They were to live in forests, not in cities, and their only shelter was to be the shadow of a tree. There they were to sit, to spread their carpet, but not to lie down, not even in sleep! "

These austerities I cannot find are ever practised at Ceylon at present.

14. Compare BURNS:

> "Her prentice han' she tried on man,
> An' then she made the lasses O !"

16. MENIKHĀMI, the Lady Jewel, is a name still frequent among Kandyan women, though no longer among the higher classes.

17. ELU is ancient Sinhalese, less Sanskritised than the modern. This poem is in Elu.

Native works have no spaces between the words, and no stop or pause, or mark of punctuation whatever, except the period. Hence, to be able to read aloud, pausing only at the proper places, implies a thorough acquaintance with the text.

Thanks to the gratuitous services of the priests, who teach children at the *pansalas*, or schools attached to the temples, ability to read and write their own language is a common accomplishment among the Sinhalese.

The last two lines of the seventeenth stanza in the translation belong in the original to the eighteenth. It is the only instance in which the version does not read, stanza for stanza, with the original. What is translated *dark*, is, literally, *blue* or *dark blue*.

INDRA, or SAKRA, the regent of the gods, is represented as a white man, sitting upon the elephant *Airāvan*, and holding in one hand the thunderbolt, in the other his bow. He is said to have a thousand eyes, the origin of which myth, though given with great minuteness in Hindu legends, need not be repeated here. SAKRA will be found one of the principal characters in the poem, a veritable *Deus ex machinā*.

19. The author was Mohottāla, or Writer in the household of ATTANĀYAKA, the husband of MENIKHĀMI.

20. MERU, the sacred mountain, the Olympus of Oriental mythology, is, as will be seen in the sequel, repeatedly alluded to by

Eastern writers. It is said to stand in the centre, or, as others hold, to the northward of JAMBUDWÎPA ; and to be scores of thousands of miles in height and circumference. A stone let fall from the top would take more than four months in reaching the earth ! On the summit is the abode of SAKRA, described in the note to the fourth stanza. Like all other sentient beings, its occupants, gods though they be, are liable to change and decay.

MAHA MERU is, on the east, of a silver colour ; south-east, pale blue ; south, sapphire ; south-west, blue ; west, coral ; north-west, red gold ; north, gold ; north-east, virgin gold! Between it and the great girdle of rocks that surrounds the earth, are (see the thirty-second stanza) seven concentric circles of rocks enclosing the six great oceans. One of the oceans, being white as milk, is called the MILKY SEA. It is frequently alluded to in the poem.

21. This stanza, the last of the Prelude, is evidently offered by way of propitiation to the critics.

22. DAMBADIVA or JAMBUDWÎPA, India. The city SEVET, or SRASVATI, is held to be identical with Gaya in Bahar, round which, for miles and miles, large masses of ruins are still to be found. Frequent allusion is made to the city in Buddhistic legends, as having been one of the places where GAUTAMA BUDDHA principally lived, and taught his followers. One of the monasteries in the city, that built by the wealthy merchant, ANÊPIDU, or ANATHAPIN-DADA, is described in the forty-second stanza. The remains, it is said, can still be traced.

25. What in the translation is rendered fair-eyed, or beautiful-eyed, is literally, in the original, long-eyed. A long, or, as we would say, almond-shaped eye, appears to have been considered a great beauty.

26. What is called at home, " the man in the moon," is by the Sinhalese termed " the hare in the moon ; " and the following legend is told regarding it. The Bôdisat, in one of his transmigrations, was born a hare. He was asked for food by a hungry man (a god in disguise), and replied that he had nothing to give but his own flesh. He then caused a fire to be lit, and threw himself into it to be roasted. In perpetual remembrance of this act of devotion and self-sacrifice for the good of others, the figure of a hare was placed in the moon.

29. *The monarch of our woods.* Literally, *she-elephant.* The Nā-tree is the ironwood-tree. The crimson-tipped leaves on the top-most boughs of this noble forest tree are very striking and beau-tiful. So too are the flowers.

30. In this and the following stanza, and indeed throughout the poem, where similes are brought in, care, it will be observed, is taken, sometimes to a wearisome extent, " to explain the metaphor by a statement of the comparison." This is laid down as essen-tially necessary according to Sinhalese canons of criticism.

34. The Titans, *A surs*, an order of beings of supernatural strength, stature, and powers, and antagonistic to the *Dēvas* or gods. They are reputed to live under Meru. They were defeated by SAKRA ; and have ever since been kept in subjection. This is, no doubt, the original of the Greek myth. One of the most celebrated of the *Asurs* was RĀHU, as to whom see the note appended to the ninety-eighth stanza.

40. *The three royal prerogatives*—power to inflict punishment, great personal energy, command of counsel.

The four schemes of statecraft—force, punishment, diplomacy, intrigue.

The seven graces, or embellishments of administration, rendering the throne illustrious and powerful—1. Prime Minister ; 2. An Ally ; 3. Treasure ; 4. Territory ; 5. A Stronghold ; 6. An Army ; 7. People.

The ten kingly virtues — uprightness, practice of pious obser-vances, almsgiving, tenderness, compassion, patience, evenness of temper, liberality in presents, peacefulness, addiction to religious austerities.

The four rules of guidance, or four chief moral virtues—alms-giving, affability, promoting the welfare of others, and *loving others as ourselves.*

52. Within the open quadrangle of a wihára, surrounded by the cloisters of the monks, the Preaching Hall generally stands, and contains, at one end, a colossal figure of BUDDHA, either in a stand-ing, sitting, or recumbent attitude. A good specimen of a Buddhist monastery, as existing at the present day in Ceylon, is to be seen in the Malwatta Wihára ("The Flower-garden Monastery ") at Kandy, on the margin of the Kandy Lake, and occupying a strik-ingly beautiful site in that most picturesque of Eastern towns.

It may not be out of place to add that this Wihára and that of Asgiriya (the latter about a mile from Kandy), are the two universities, so to speak, to which every priest of orthodox Buddhism in Ceylon should be affiliated. At both Wiháras the priests are very courteous to visitors. The Kandyan Kings were accustomed to provide entertainment for foreign devotees and other guests at various religious buildings, set apart and endowed with lands for the purpose, near the town. One of the best known of these, the Gangaráma Wihára, is near the Lewéla Ferry, about a mile and a half from Kandy, and is rendered remarkable by a colossal statue of BUDDHA, standing, carved out of the solid granitic rock, on the face of which rock, outside the building, is inscribed, moreover, the title-deed conveying the lands granted to the Wihára. Though no longer a royal *hospitium*, the Wihára sees merry guests and festive gatherings still, and many a pleasant picnic is held in or near its wood-embowered precincts.

It is said King WIMALADHARMA invited upwards of two thousand foreign priests to Kandy on the occasion of the removal of the tooth.

At Mulgirigala, in Hambantota district, is another Buddhist monastery of great repute, to which reference is made further on.

55. BUDDHA'S abode on earth was, according to the legends, fragrant with the choicest perfumes. The *Sidat Sangaráva*, a classic work on grammar, begins thus : " Bow ye to the feet of Buddha ! Having made my heart *a scented house* for him who saw the perfection of all things, I have composed this work."

57. According to Buddhistic legends, the manner in which the Great Teacher walked excited universal admiration (*Manual of Buddhism*, p. 366). If there were thorns, rocks, or other hindrances, they removed themselves; if mud, it dried up; if holes, they became level and smooth as the top of a drum ; if elevations, they melted away like butter that sees fire ; and the air was filled with choice and delicate perfumes ! If he passed anybody in pain, the pain, however intense, ceased instantly; and when his foot touched the ground a lotus sprang up at every step ! His foot came down as lightly as cotton wool ! He could walk in a space not larger than a mustard seed ; and yet, with as much ease as a man may cross his doorstep, he, on one occasion, placed his foot on the earth, then on the rock, Yugandhára, then on the top of Meru !

The so-called impression of his footstep on Adam's Peak, Srīpā-dakanda, "the Mountain of the Holy Foot," in Ceylon, is visited by thousands of pilgrims every year. Singularly enough, while the Buddhist reverences the mark as the footprint of the Founder of his faith, Hindus connect it with Sivā, and Mahometans all over the East believe it to be that of Adam, the great progenitor of the human race, whence its name! For a most interesting work on Adam's Peak and the various traditions connected with that sacred mount, the reader is referred to Mr SKEEN's *Adam's Peak*, published in Ceylon in 1870. See also Mr A. M. FERGUSON's attractive *Souvenirs of Ceylon*.

60. The fruit of the nuga (*ficus Bengalensis*) tree is of a yellowish-red colour. The orthodox colour for priests' robes is either saffron, or bright red, the hue of the pomegranate flower. The saffron dye is generally obtained by boiling fresh chips of jakwood, newly cut; and is done by the priests themselves.

61. BUDDHA is always represented as having his whole body en-circled by six rays, or, so to speak, *nimbi*, of the colours named in the text, blue, golden, red, white, brownish-red, and composite. There is also what may be described as a crest of rays springing from his head.
A curious phenomenon occasionally seen in Ceylon, consisting of a narrow band of pure white, spanning the sky, is called by the Sinhalese, "Buddha's rays." This is seen in May or June.
According to the *Pujavaliya*, the light that shone from BUDDHA's body, as he went from place to place, was like the splendour of gems in a royal diadem, or a canopy adorned with gold and silver, or a garland of the most beautiful flowers, or a hall filled with the sweetest blossoms and odours!

64. The garden tree named is the *Wada*, which bears a beautiful flower, generally of a bright red, and grows in great profusion near religious buildings. The offerings laid in front of the shrines in Buddhist temples in Ceylon consist of this and of sweet-scented flowers, which are renewed every day. Of the *wada-mal*, some species bear pale yellow, pink, and, according to *Stocqueler's Orien-tal Interpreter*, light blue flowers.
This beautiful flower is frequently called "the shoe-flower,"

from its possessing the property of polishing leather shoes! Its
services in colouring tarts and stewed fruit are also well known to
Oriental housewifery! Hamlet's exclamation to Horatio would
almost seem in point!

66. The myrobolan seed is of a brownish-red colour.

68. Iu the lowest world, the world of air, no beings live.

73. *The fire motions of reverence.*—By this is meant a mode of
prostration whereby five parts of the body touched the ground. It
consisted of kneeling and bending the head so low as to touch the
ground, the joined hands, palm to palm, being at the same time
placed on the forehead.

74. Of the thirty-two forbidden themes I am unable to obtain
any account.

77. *The Bōdisat*, the name applied to the Founder of Buddhism
before he attained the Buddhaship.

SECOND PART.

80. The city of KUSĀVATI—the exact site of which is not ascer-
tained—is described by a royal poet of Ceylon, KING PRĀKKRAMA
BĀHU III. (who ascended the throne, A.D. 1267) in his poem of
Kawsilumina, thus :—

Kusāvati was a city of renown, the birthplace of men of worth,

> ["Auld Ayr, that ilka toon surpasses,
> For honest men ! "]

the treasury of all wealth and happiness! It resembled a lotus
born in the Brahma world! Like jewelled armlets were its crystal
ramparts, the pillars of the concave heavens, which, though
stretched on the ground [rose so high as to seem to have] out-dis-
tanced those who travel in the air ! Its moat, abounding in lotuses,
the haunts of the ever-humming bee, was to the city, whose forti-
fications it surrounded, as a girdle round the waist of a woman !
(*Introd. to Sidat Sangarāra*, p. 170.)

81. KAILASA, a mountain (understood to be one of the Himalayan range) fabled as the abode of KUWERA, the god of wealth, and
a favourite retreat of SIVĀ.

> " By strong desire through all he makes his way,
> Till Siva's seat appears ! . . . . Behold Mount Kailasay ! "
> —SOUTHEY, *Curse of Kehama.*

82. *The Wishing Tree,* or, what would be more exact, *The Wish-
conferring Tree!* In Eastern mythology the *kalpatāra,* a fabulous
tree growing in INDRA's heaven, which yields whatever is desired,
and supplies the wants of all who shelter under it. It forms the
subject of the forty-fifth section of the most complete original *Silpa
Shastra* extant, as described by RAM RAZ in an essay on Hindu
Architecture, quoted by PERCIVAL, *Land of the Vedas,* p. 129.

85. The goddess LAKSHMI, like Venus in the Western Pantheon,
ranks high among Oriental myths. She was produced at the
churning of the sea. She became wife of VISHNU, and goddess of
beauty and good fortune. In Ceylon, the name commonly applied
to her, is SRIYAKANTĀVA.

89. No explanation is obtainable as to what is meant by particu-
larising the tusks on the right-hand side, as is done in the text.

93. *The five sorts of music* are said to be the five tones or kinds of
music produced from the various sorts of tom-toms, or native drums,
each yielding a different sound. Tom-toms are used to accompany
dancing, singing, and performances on wind instruments. (See
SKEEN'S *Adam's Peak,* p. 157 and 319.)

In all directions is, literally, in the original, " in the *ten* directions," which are thus enumerated : east, west, north, south,
north-east, south-east, south-west, north-west, the point above the
zenith, and that under the nadir.

94. Here is introduced the cardinal doctrine of Buddhism, and
of Hinduism as well, that the merit or demerit beings accumulate
in their various transmigrations has the effect of bettering or
debasing their after-condition. See note to the concluding stanza
of the Sixth Part.

96. In the original, this admired stanza runs thus (colons being
put between the several words) :—

SEDA : KARAWEYI : DININDU :
MASIN : MASE : ADUWEYI : INDU :
NALA : WEDE : SELEYI : SINDU :
EYIN : UVAMEK : KONDA : ME : RAJA : BANDU.

98. Ráhu was a noted *Asur* (Titan), living in the Nâga World.
When the gods assembled to churn the sea and produce the *amrita*,
the nectar or water of life, out of which LAKSHMI sprang, RÁHU
went secretly to the spot and obtained a draught, by which he
became immortal. The Sun and Moon, who were present guarding
the nectar, reported the theft to VISHNU, who cut RÁHU's body in
two. Having been rendered immortal, however, the head and
trunk, though severed, remained alive, and were translated to the
sky, as RÁHU and KETU respectively. RÁHU cherishes vindictive
animosity against the Sun and Moon for betraying him, and
endeavours to destroy them! The seizure of them in his mouth
is the cause of eclipses! The belief that eclipses are caused by a
huge, supernatural monster swallowing the sun, is shared by
nations widely remote from each other, among others by the Chinese
and the Greenlanders. In China during an eclipse, drums are
beaten, and horrible noises made to frighten the monster, and
make him disgorge his prey! The churning of the sea is described
with great minuteness in the *Mahabharata*.

100. The five feminine charms or graces (*panchakalyâna*) so
often alluded to in Sinhalese verse, are said to be—red lips, long,
soft hair, white regular teeth, soft and blooming skin, *and youth!*

101. SÍLAVATI, the Decorous Lady. PRABAVATI signifies the
Lustrous Maiden, or Lady of Light : JAYANPATI, the Victorious
Lord.

114. The suggestion made by the citizens hardly seems likely to
bring *the King* an heir. All over the East, however, it is to be
remembered, adoption is held of almost equal consideration with
actual relationship by blood.

129. *Heaven's high town*, literally, "*the City of the Thirty-three*,"
alluding to the thirty-three eminent personages, who, on account of
their great holiness, went straight from earth to Swarga, and
became divine. SAKRA or INDRA is at the head of these, and is
thence called, as in the text, *The King of Gods*. According to the

tenets of Hinduism, the inferior gods dwelling in Indra's heaven are *three hundred and thirty millions* in number, and are divided into classes and hierarchies of every conceivable grade. As Dr Duff eloquently says in his work on India : " All the virtues and the vices of man ; all the allotments of life, beauty, jollity, and sport ; the hopes and fears of youth ; the felicities and misfortunes of man-hood; the joys and sorrows of old age—all, all are placed under the presiding influence of superior powers ! Every scene, every element, and almost every object in nature : the bud that bursts forth in spring, the blossom of summer, and the fruits of autumn ; meadow and grove, fountain and stream, hill and valley, all have their guardian genii, whose freaks and revelries greatly outstrip in number and variety ' the fairy gambols and goblin feats ' recog-nised by the credulity of Northern superstition."

Sakra's seat of rocks, alluded to in the 128th and 523th stanzas, is said to grow hot when misery and suffering take place on earth, in order to warn the god, who is believed to render help and consola-tion to beings in distress.

136. "*Here did we dwell of yore.*"—The statement does not appear to have had any foundation in fact !

137. Betel (in Bengali, *paun* or *paunsoparee ;* Sinh., *bulat*). The leaf of the betel plant, a kind of pepper, is universally chewed among the Sinhalese, who invariably carry a portion with them in their betel-pouches, and rarely indeed are without a quid in their mouths. It is smeared with *chunam* (lime), moistened with water, and some cardamum seeds, tobacco, and a portion of the nut of the areka-palm, taken with it. The *chunam* renders the saliva of a blood-red colour ; and the effect of the mastication is to discolour and blacken the teeth. The smell of the betel leaf greatly re-sembles that of parsley. It is highly thought of by the Sinhalese : and its praises are thus sung in the *Hitopadesa :* " Betel is pungent, bitter, spicy, sweet, alkaline, astringent; a carminative, a destroyer of phlegm, a vermifuge, a sweetener of the breath, an ornament of the mouth (!), a remover of impurities, and a kindler of the flame of love ! O friend ! these thirteen properties of betel are hard to be met with, even in heaven ! "

143. " *What better is than wisdom, Sire, in all the world beside ?* "—

O

There is a striking little Sinhalese poem in the *Kawminimaldama*
("Garland of Poetical Gems"), written by KATUWANA MUHANDIRAM
in 1770, which, with a rendering into English, may be quoted
here.

PIRISIDU KULEHI MUT
RATIHIMI SADISI RUWĘTAT
PURADURU SE NĘNĘTAT
UGAT SIP NĘTA SEBEHI NOHOBIT

DILINDU KULA UPANAT
RUSIRU WISULUWA WUWAT
MANĀ SIP DATA HOT
MAHARU NIRINDŌ PAWĀ E PUDAT ·

YAHA PANDURU LŌPAL
KISI KALA NOWĒ EKATUL
DESA PUDATA LŌPAL
WIYAT DASA DESA PUDAT HĘMAKAL.
—ALWIS, *Introd. Sidat. Sang.*, p. 230.

Though born of high descent, and decked
  With INDRA's skill and KĀMA's grace,
Without a polished intellect
  No man may win distinguished place.

Yet though he owns no golden store,
  His form uncouth, and low his birth,
f his the wealth of wisdom's lore,
  Great kings will dignify his worth

For royalty, however great,
  To wisdom still inferior stands.
A king sways but his narrow state:
  Genius a boundless realm commands !

The second stanza bears a resemblance to HORACE (Od. ii. 18).

"At fides et ingeni
  Benigna vena est : pauperemque dives,
Me petit."

Honour and genius both are mine':
  With these, a will untaught to waver.
Even nobles bow at learning's shrine,
  And rich men court the poet's favour.

144. *Kusa*, a sacred grass. The word *Kusa* in Sinhalese, besides
being the name of a king and of a region of the earth, signifies the
womb (whence, apparently, our hero's name), the breast, a sacrificial grass, a rope, wrought iron, a halter, a bridle, weak, depraved,

mad! As to the sacrificial grass, a Brahman is said to have given
a handful to BUDDHA, who cast it on the ground under a Bō-tree,
where it was immediately transformed into a seat for him. The
Bō-tree (*ficus religiosa*) is the sacred tree so greatly honoured
among Buddhists; and, when growing near a temple, the object of
scrupulous care. It resembles an aspen, though of much statelier
and larger growth. Can the European myth attached to the aspen
have, on account of this resemblance, been in any way derived
from the many legends associated with this sacred tree? The
belief current in many European countries, notably Scotland and
the North of England, as to the magical properties of the rowan-tree
or mountain ash, is said to be owing to its resemblance to a tree
held sacred among the primitive forefathers of Indo-European races,
the Aryans. To revert to Bō-trees, the historical one at ANURÁDHA-
PURA, in Ceylon, is reputed to be upwards of two thousand years
old! Of this famous tree, FERGUSSON (*Tree and Serpent Worship*)
observes: " The transfer of a branch of the Bō-tree from Buddha-
gaya to Anurádhapura is as authentic and important as any event
recorded in the annals of Ceylon. Sent by ASOKA, 250 B.C., it was
received with the utmost reverence by DEVANAMPIYATISSO, and
planted in the most conspicuous spot in the centre of his capital.
There it has been reverenced as the chief and most important
' numen' of Ceylon for more than two thousand years: and it, or
its lineal descendant, sprung at least from the old root, is there
worshipped at this hour. The city is in ruins: its great dāgobas
have fallen into decay : its monasteries have disappeared ; but the
great Bō-tree still flourishes, according to the legend—ever green,
never growing or decreasing, but living on for ever, for the delight
and worship of mankind! Annually thousands repair to the sacred
precincts within which it stands to do it honour."

THIRD PART.

158. " *The Eye of the Three Worlds* "—the worlds, respectively,
of gods, men, and asurs. This title is frequently applied to
BUDDHA.

165. According to the Eastern code of politeness, an inferior should address a superior, not face to face, but remaining a little at one side.

167. The life of a hermit, being considered best suited for holy meditation and mortification of earthly desires, is held up to especial honour in Buddhistic works. Was this view borrowed from Buddhism by the early followers of Christianity?

183. It is of interest to note that all through the poem, the Queen appears invested with more power than is usually accorded to her sex among Eastern nations. It must be remembered, however, that Ceylon had, at dates anterior to that of the poem, been ruled more than once by a Queen : and that wives, at least among the higher classes, have more authority in Sinhalese households than almost anywhere else in Asia. By Kandyan law, indeed, the rights of married people are put on a perfect equality, or rather, if ˙ anything, the wife's transcend those of the husband. Nowhere, unless perhaps among the Eskimoes, is a married woman so thoroughly independent as is a Kandyan wife.

The respectful term used in addressing or speaking of a Sin-halese lady, is " The Master of the Mansion ! "

The dispatching of the golden statue, as hinted in a previous note, was probably suggested by the Embassy to Portugal.

196. This seems a fair specimen of hyperbole, new, and, perhaps, not too immoderate.

198. With the ancients, though the opinion is opposed to modern English views and canons of taste, it is clear the poet con-sidered a narrow brow a great feminine beauty—" an excellent thing in woman." See also the 549th stanza.

199. ' Long leaves darkly *blue*.'—In Sinhalese, the same word, *nil*, signifies both blue and green : and to this day, to describe the latter, as distinguished from blue, a roundabout expression, "leaf-colour," has to be used. The translation might, therefore, read either darkly blue or darkly green ; but the former is, I think, more consonant with what the poet sought to convey.

The question is one as to the colour of eyebrows : as to the colour of eyes, it may be noted, that the native races of Ceylon are never blue-eyed.

202. Among Kandyan women a wheel-shaped ornament, almost as large as a rupee, and let into the lobe of the ear, is very generally worn. The bright metal being reflected on the smooth cheek, would make the ornaments seem four in number.

Kāma, the Indian Cupid, is represented as a handsome youth, the most beautiful being in the three worlds, riding on a lory or parrot, and holding in his hands his bow strung with bees, and arrows tipped with flowers. He is always accompanied by his wife, Rati, by spring and gentle breezes, by the cuckoo and the bee.

203. Siva's wife, the goddess Durga, or Parvati, or Kali, the most popular of all the Hindu goddesses. Calcutta takes its name from her. In it alone, Ward says, it is computed not less than half a million sterling is spent yearly on the occasion of the festival in her honour! In the worship of the goddess Kali, Hindu superstition exhibits itself in its most revolting form. As Mr Trevelyan (*Letters of a Competition Wallah*) remarks, the revelries and bacchanalian orgies that take place during the *Durga Puja* bring vividly before the beholder what may be believed to have characterised the worship of Bacchus in Greece.

The three rare marks of grace (kambugrīvā).—According to Clough, this, signifying a neck marked with three lines like a shell, is considered indicative of exalted fortune, and a sign of great beauty.

204. The champak-tree and its sweet-scented yellow flower are themes of perpetual allusion in Oriental poetry, of which Moore was not forgetful in *Lalla Rookh*—a poem enthusiastically admired by Easterns acquainted with English. Most readers will also remember Shelley's exquisite *Lines to an Indian Air*—

> "The wandering airs they faint
> On the dark and silent stream :
> The champak odours fall
> Like sweet thoughts in a dream !

The nightingale's complaint
:   It dies upon her heart,
      As I must on thine,
          Beloved as thou art ! "

206. In places in this and the following stanzas, so minutely descriptive of PRABAVATI'S personal charms, it has been thought
right to deviate occasionally from strict literal fidelity in the translation.   But the changes made involve in no case a wide departure
from the original.

What is meant by the Northern Sea is, no doubt, the ocean to
the north of MERU.

213. The *hansa*, the swan, or goose—for the latter is, perhaps, the
more faithful translation—is often alluded to.   It is the *vahan* or
vehicle of BRAHMA.   As a royal bird, it is often to be found sculp-
tured on the remains of the palaces occupied by different Kings of
Ceylon.

226. This is in allusion to her name, PRABAVATI, the Lustrous
Maiden, or Lady of Light.

229. The *wandurá*, or, as it is sometimes, but erroneously, called,
wandaru, the large black monkey, which abounds in Ceylon forests
and jungles.   It is easily tamed, and, when tamed, very affectionate,
though by no means prepossessing.

237. *Bold as a lion*, or voiced as a lion.   Either rendering is
correct.

FOURTH PART.

245. *The white umbrella* was, in the East, regarded as one of
the chief insignia of royalty.   At this day the device on the royal
seal of the Kings of Siam is a sevenfold umbrella.   This is affixed
not only to state documents, but also to private letters, some of
which latter the writer has had opportunities of seeing, as the
Second King, a prince of considerable attainments, was, a few years

ago, in the habit of corresponding in English with a Government officer at Galle. Between Siam and Ceylon a close connection has long been kept up, on account chiefly of the identity of religion. See also allusion to the white umbrella in reference to King PRĀK-KRAMA BĀHU VI., uniting the whole of Ceylon into one kingdom, in the *Sela Lihini Sandēsē* ("The Sela's Message"), a classic Sinhalese poem, an able and scholarly translation of which, with notes and glossary, by Mr W. C. MACREADY, of the Ceylon Civil Service, was published at Colombo in 1867.

246. A kalpa is said to be the measure of the duration of the world previous to its next renewal—the process of destruction and renewal being destined to go on for ever! The length of a kalpa is 432 millions of years! At the close, the world is to be destroyed three times in succession—by rain, by wind, and, finally, by fire. Phœnix-like, however, it is to rise, fresh and young again, from its ashes.

247. The first line expresses what Easterns consider a fully equipped army, *chaturanga*—literally, "the fourfold force," an array consisting of cavalry, infantry, elephants, and chariots. It is hardly necessary to add, that chess takes its name from *chaturanga*, itself being a mimic battle with all the four forces employed. The game, tradition asserts, owes its origin to Ceylon—Ceylon of the prehistoric era—having been invented during the tedious siege of Sri Lankapura, the capital of Lanka, the Troy of the great Eastern Epic, the *Rāmayana*. Lanka is the native name for Ceylon.

258. Allusion to the prevalence of a custom of this kind among many nations will be found in Sir JOHN LUBBOCK's *Origin of Civilisation. Savages.* p. 56.

263. Thus in the original :—

> MINISUN HIRAGEWALA
> SIYATUN SAHA MĘDIRIWALA
> BENDI SIŢI DAMWALA
> MIDU SIWUPĀ KĘLAN EMAKALA.

264. On festive occasions in Ceylon the practice of putting up triumphal arches, generally decorated with great taste, is very

common. The effect is often very striking. Fruit and flowers
now-a-days take the place of the gold and gems in the text, and,
there can be no question, with a much more picturesque effect.
The arches put up on the occasion of H.R.H. THE DUKE OF EDIN-
BURGH'S visit to the island, in 1870, were extremely tasteful. For
a spirited description of the Prince's visit, and the sport in the
forests, the reader is refered to Mr CAPPER's interesting book, *The
Duke of Edinburgh in Ceylon.*

266. This stanza records the abdication of King OKĀVAS, in favour
of his son KUSA, who would seem to have assumed imperial sway
immediately on his marriage.

————

FIFTH PART.

267. RATI, the wife of KĀMA, the God of Love.

278. Elephant keepers are, in Ceylon, a class by themselves; and
are said to justify to this day the Queen's opinion of them. Their
authority, however, over the huge beasts they control is very
marked. It is singular how comparatively large a vocabulary of
articulate words the elephant acquires a knowledge of. In an in-
vestigation held before the writer as to the decease of a spectator
who was trodden to death by a enraged elephant during one of the
nightly processions at Kandy in 1864, evidence was given to the
effect, that between twenty and thirty articulated words—not in-
terjectional merely, and not of the vernacular tongue—are in common use in speaking to elephants, each having a distinct meaning,
such as " Strike a man ! " " Strike a tree ! " " Kneel ! " " Drag ! "
" Move on this or that side," and the like. This of itself may be
regarded as proof of the high sagacity of the animal.

293. Jaggery (Sinh., *hakuru*) is the sugar made by boiling down
the sweet juice (*toddy*) extracted from the spathe of the flower of
the kitul or jaggery palm. Hakuru, sometimes written sakuru (*h*

and *s* being nearly always interchangeable in Sinhalese), is unmistakeably the word from which sugar (*saccharum, sucre, zucker*) is derived.

310. The Indian cuckoo (*kōkilā*) is a bird of black plumage. Its note is pleasing, and, according to Eastern poetry, where it often figures, productive of great emotion. Like its European namesake, it is reared in the nest of birds other than its parents, whose own nestlings it summarily gets rid of.

312. This stanza in the original, quoted below, is a great favourite in Sinhalese households, and especially, it is said, among mothers, who commit the passage to memory, and are fond of repeating it.

> **E VUYANA LIYA LIYAN TURU HIMI VALANDIMINA**
> **LELADENA ATU ATIN SĀ MUVA SUTAN GENA**
> **SUPIPENA LATA LAVAN YUT KUSUMAN VATINA**
> **NALAVANA VEṆNA BINGU SAN SURATAL BASINA.**

313. Nā, the ironwood tree (*mesua ferrea*), has already been noticed in a previous note, as has also the champak. The flower of the ironwood is sweet scented, and often forms part of the morning offerings at Buddhist temples. The mango is sufficiently well known to English readers. The jak (Sinh., *kos ;* botanically, *artocarpus integrifolia*) is a handsome tree, plentiful in Ceylon, of the same species as the bread-fruit (also plentiful), valuable both for its timber, which is of excellent quality, and much used for furniture and all kinds of carpentry, and its large fruit, a staple article of diet, whether raw or curried, among the poorer classes. The fruit grows straight out of the stem, and sometimes attains an enormous size, while as many as sixty or seventy, at various stages of growth, may occasionally be seen upon a good tree at one and the same time.

It is highly thought of by Sinhalese villagers, one of whom (two of his jak-trees having been cut down to admit the passage of the telegraph wire, some years ago, when Ceylon was first put in connection with the Indian telegraph system) characteristically told the writer that the loss of each was to him almost as great a bereavement as the death of a child, indeed, in some respects, rather more so, as other children might be born to him in his lifetime, but such stately trees as he had been deprived of could not possibly grow up before he died!

The jambu, or Malay apple, is a handsome, well-shaped tree, growing to the height of about forty feet. The leaves are about a foot long, by four inches broad. The flower is bright pink; the fruit, not unlike a pear in shape, juicy, and not ill-flavoured. It is sometimes red, sometimes white with a tinge of red.

316. *Fiend :* in the original, *yakā.* The yakās are not (*Manual of Buddhism,* p. 44) to be classed with devils, though this is their popular designation. The Sinhalese have a great dread of their power; and in times of distress, the devil-dancer (*yakādura*) is frequently called in to overcome the malignity of the fiends by his chants and dances and charms. When a patient is dangerously ill, and ordinary remedies are of no avail, the dancers are sent for; and in the sick-room, often crowded to suffocation, they perform from dusk to dawn their heathenish ceremonies, consisting mostly of violent posturing, gestures, singing, and the slaying of an animal, generally a cock, by way of propitiation or sacrifice. These ceremonies receive no sanction from Buddhism, though almost universally practised. They are probably a remnant of the most ancient worship ever practised in the island. *Yakās* are not spirits condemned to torment, nor is their abode in the various hells. Some live on earth and in the waters, and others even form part of the guard round *Swarga.* They marry. They delight in dances and other amusements. They are of enormous strength; and some possess great splendour and dignity.

There is a story found in one of the most popular legends in the *Book of the Five Hundred and Fifty Births,* the *Umandāva* or *Um-magga Jātakē* (a prose work which, it may be remarked, is one of the books prescribed by the Board of Examiners in Ceylon), relative to a *yakinni* or she-fiend, that may be interesting to English readers from its striking resemblance to a passage in Scripture (1 KINGS iii. 16-28).

The passage, slightly condensed, is given below. It is to be premised that the Pandit is the Bōdisat in the transmigration wherein he became Chief Councillor of King VĒDĒHA of Miyulu. The story runs thus:—

A woman came with her child to the Pandit's pond to bathe,

and leaving him on the bank, went down into the water. As soon as she had done so, a she-fiend (*yakinni*), in the guise of a woman, seeing the child, and wishing to devour it, came up and said, "Friend, is this pretty babe yours? May I nurse it?" The mother replied "Well!" upon which the yakinni, taking the child and nursing him a little while, ran off with him. The mother pursued, screaming for her son and expostulating, while the yakinni boldly cried: "Where didst thou own a child? It is mine!" Whilst the quarrel went on, they came near the Pandit's Hall; and the Pandit hearing the disturbance, asked what was the matter. He, seeing that one of the disputants was a yakinni, by reason of the non-twinkling of her eyes and their redness, which was as the redness of two olinda seeds (*abrus precatorius*), said, "Will you abide by my judgment?" They assented. He then had a line drawn on the ground, and the child laid upon it; and, telling the yakinni to seize its arms, and the mother its legs, said, "He shall be adjudged son of her who pulls him off." They pulled accordingly; and as the child writhed with pain, the mother, sorely grieving, let him go, and stood apart and wept.

Then the Bōdisat asked the bystanders, "Whose hearts are tender to their children? those of mothers, or those of persons who are not mothers?" They replied, "O Pandit! Mothers' hearts are tender!" Then said he, "Which, think you, is the mother? She who has the child now, or she who let it go?" Many answered, "She who let it go is the mother!" The Pandit then told them how he knew one of the disputants was a yakinni, rebuked and admonished her, and administered to her the five *sil* [see note to the twelfth stanza], restored the child to his mother, and sent her rejoicing away!

[See the story told at greater length among the tales at the end of the volume. The story is believed not to be traceable to a Hebrew source.]

SIXTH PART.

336. The PASÊMUNIS or PASÊBUDDHAS were inferior teachers, who frequently appeared in the world before the birth of GAUTAMA BUDDHA. Although they were ascetics, and practised the observances that led to NIRVÂNA, they attained that consummation without the prerogatives peculiar to a BUDDHA, and rendered little or no spiritual help to others.

According to HARDY, the PASÊBUDDHAS are sages of wondrous power, who never appear at the same time as a supreme Buddha. They attain to their high privileges by their own unaided powers. They rank between the supreme Buddha and the Rahats, which latter are those who have entered on the fourth path leading to Nirvâna, and become free from evil desire and cleaving to all sensuous objects. Alms given to a PASÊMUNI earn one hundred times as much merit as those given to a Rahat. Hence, perhaps, the wondrous efficacy of the ghee mentioned in the course of this canto ¦ The PASÊMUNIS cannot release any other being from the miseries of successive existence.

342. Ghee, clarified butter, is held of more account in the East than might at first sight appear. The Hindus maintain that Maha Brahma created the Brahmans and the cow at the same time : the former to read the Vedas, the latter to yield milk, and ghee for offerings. The gods, by partaking of the burnt-offerings, are said to enjoy exquisite pleasure : and men, by eating ghee, destroy their sins ! (WARD, i. p. 249).

353. A yodun is said to be equivalent to four gows, say, from fifteen to sixteen miles.

357. This stanza embodies the moral of the book, and indeed a chief, if not *the* chief precept Buddhism teaches—the acquirement of merit or demerit by the deeds done in successive transmigrations. Hinduism inculcates the same. "The spirit now conditioned as a man, or even a being of higher auspices, may become a blade of grass, a shrub, a mineral, an insect, a nymph, a god !" The doctrine of rewards and punishments is, indeed, a psychological principle that must at all times have occupied the minds of thinking men of all

countries, races, and opinions. That it did so among the Jews, may be gathered from the question put by the disciples to Our SAVIOUR (St John ix. 2) : "Who did sin, this man or his parents, that he was *born blind?*" In the answer Our SAVIOUR gave, Christians, blessed by the ineffable radiance of the Divine Light, with which the teachings accepted by others cannot for a moment be compared, may with rejoicing receive comfort such as can never be derived from the vague and vain dreams of pagan creeds and systems of philosophy.

The views entertained by philosophic Hinduism are given at length in a striking passage put into the mouth of Krishna, in the celebrated epic, the *Mahabharata*, of which passage a portion has been rendered unto verse as under :—

"The truly wise should never mourn, should never vainly cherish woe,
For those who live or those who die, who hence upon their journey go !
When I, or yonder kings, were not, such time was not, nor e'er could be;
Nor shall the hour to bid us cease come ever unto them or me !
The spirit, clad in changing guise, speeds on through childhood, youth,
    and age,
Then, in another form renewed, renews again its pilgrimage ! "

The remainder of the passage is very remarkable. As quoted by Southey, in a note appended to *The Curse of Kehama*, it runs thus : "The soul is not a thing of which a man may say, it hath been, is about to be, or is to be hereafter ; for it is a thing without birth, it is ancient, constant, eternal, and is not to be destroyed in this its mortal frame." Compare Wordsworth's noble ode—

" Our birth is but a sleep and a forgetting :
    The soul that rises with us, our life's star,
        Hath had elsewhere its setting,
            And cometh from afar ;
        Not in entire forgetfulness,
        And not in utter nakedness,
    But trailing clouds of glory do we come
        From GOD, Who is our home !

.   .   .   .

    Hence in a season of calm weather,
        Though inland far we be,
    Our souls have sight of that immortal Sea
        Which brought us hither ;
    Can in a moment travel thither,
    And see the children sport upon the shore,
    And hear the mighty waters rolling evermore ! "

But to revert to the quotation : " How can the man who believes the soul is incorruptible, eternal, inexhaustible, and without birth, think that he can either kill it or cause it to be killed ? As a man throws away old garments and puts on new, even so the soul, having quitted its old mortal frames, entereth into others which are new. The weapon divides it not, nor fire burneth, nor doth water dissolve it, nor wind dry it up ! For it is invisible, inconsumable, incorruptible, and is not to be dried up ; it is eternal, universal, permanent, immovable ; it is invisible, inconceivable, and unalterable."

In illustration of the text, the following extract from the chapter on the *Ontology of Buddhism* (p. 395), as explanatory of the views held by Buddhists, deserves a place :—" Uttering the sentiments of a Buddhist, a man might say—I regard myself as a sentient being, now existing in the world of men. But I have existed in a similar manner in many myriads of previous births ; and may have passed through all possible states of being. I am now under the influence of all that I have ever done in all those ages. This is my KARMA, the arbiter of my destiny. Until I attain NIRVÁNA, I must still continue to exist ; but the states of being into which I shall pass, I cannot tell. The future is shrouded in darkness impenetrable." . . . " No sentient being can tell in what state the karma he possesses will appoint his next birth, though he may be now, and continue till death, one of the most meritorious of men. In that karma there may be the crime of murder, committed ages ago, but not yet expiated; and in the next existence, its punishment may have to be endured. There will ultimately be a reward for that which is good ; but it may be long delayed."

SEVENTH PART.

360. The last line is simply a roundabout way of saying that the King was distracted with love. This stanza and the nine next succeeding are much admired in the original.

363. The sun at a kalpa's close, when the whole world is to be destroyed by fire, will be hidden and swallowed up in raging flames.

368. The inner walls of Buddhist temples, all over the island, are covered with frescoes illustrative of the various legends, which often exhibit both spirit and taste.

EIGHTH PART.

393. There is more mention of music in the poem than one would expect from the present state of the Divine Art among the Sinhalese, whose chief instruments consist of various tom-toms, clashing cymbals, and ear-piercing fifes. The tom-toms and fifes, being in service every night at the Temple of The Tooth at Kandy, effectually accomplish there for a while what the last line of the stanza says King Kusa's guitar did at Sāgala!

400. *Chatties* are earthenware pitchers and bowls, largely used in cooking. It is worth noting that all the handicrafts the Bōdisat devoted himself to—goldsmith, stableman, potter, matmaker, and cook—are those practised by people of inferior caste. Possibly there may be some moral object covertly aimed at in this : for instance, the inculcation of the lesson that no caste however low, no occupation however slavish, is a barrier to good and meritorious conduct.

401. *A pingo* or katli is a piece of wood shaped somewhat like a bow, and laid across the shoulder to carry burdens, one of which is hung at each end; and looking, generally speaking, not unlike the conventional diagram accepted as a representation of *The Scales* in the zodiac ! It is an excellent and useful contrivance.

418. The art of cookery, Supa (whence, without question, *soup*) Sestra, occupies, as is meet, an honourable place in the roll of Eastern sciences. King Prākkrama Bāhu III., who ascended the throne of Ceylon in A.D. 1267, was, it is recorded, celebrated for his proficiency in sixty-four sciences— probably the very same attri- buted to King Kusa in the 573d stanza. In a list of such of these as equivalent English names can be ascertained for, Cookery stands twenty-fifth, coming between *Chittra*, Drawing, and *Gandharva*, Dancing and Music.

478. PRABAVATI's behaviour here described scarcely accords with what is said of her ignorance of falsehood in the 303d stanza. The Sinhalese, ungallantly enough, do not entertain a high opinion of the truthfulness of women. They have a favourite epigram, a translation of which, as under, is given in FORBES's *Eleven Years in Ceylon*. It must be premised that the udambara-tree is believed *never* to blossom.

> "I saw the udambara-tree in flower, white plumage on the crow,
> And fishes' footsteps in the deep have tracked through ebb and flow !
> If *man* it be who thus asserts, his word thou mayst believe ;
> But *never* trust a *woman's* word : *she* speaks but to deceive !"

It is only fair to add, that experience, gathered from a residence in Ceylon, whether in Government Offices or Courts of Justice, or generally, amply warrants the belief that the little weakness spoken of is by no means confined to the wayward sex alone ! The advocates of Women's Rights may also, if they choose, cite SHAKSPEARE's dictum *contra :*

> "Sigh no more, ladies, sigh no more !
> *Men* were deceivers ever !
> One foot on sea, and one on shore,
> To one thing constant never !"

490. *Conjy*, rice gruel.

506. The Homeric vigour of the Crooked Dame's manners throughout is startling, but characteristic. It may serve to illustrate the extraordinary liberties confidential servants are allowed, in even the highest Eastern households, whereof Indian history is full of examples.

NINTH PART.

529. SAKRA, like Argus, is represented as possessing a thousand eyes.

TENTH PART.

559. *Palm-flower juice*, palm wine, taree, or, as it is commonly called, *toddy*. When fresh drawn early in the morning, it is

sweet, cooling, and wholesome ; but, when fermented by the heat of the sun, becomes highly intoxicating. Arrack is distilled in Ceylon from the fermented toddy. In China and elsewhere, arrack is often made from rice. According to *Stocqueler* (*Oriental Inter-preter*, p. 223), the potent and maddening qualities of toddy are not unfrequently increased by an infusion of datura juice, which is highly narcotic and deleterious.

Toddy is extracted by slicing off the tip of the spathe of the coco-nut, or kitul-palm, flower, and placing underneath the cut an earthen pot, into which the liquor flows abundantly.

Fermented toddy is also very serviceable as yeast.

573. *The sixty-four sciences.*—Of these, the following have been enumerated, though, as will be seen, the list is far from complete. Grammar, Theology, Classical Literature, Jurisprudence, Botany, Prosody, Logic, Rhetoric, Philology, The Vedas, Mythology, Astronomy, Physiognomy, Astrology (this is still successfully cultivated in Ceylon), Medicine, Customs and Traditions, History and Biography, Fencing, Archery, Mineralogy, Drawing, Cookery, Music. Incomplete though it be, the list exhibits a goodly round of royal accomplishments.

588. *The Four Vedas* are the Rig, Yajush, Sāma, and Atharva.

The prevailing character of the ritual of the Vedas is, says Professor WILSON, the worship of the personified elements : of Agni, fire ; Indra, or the firmament; Wayu, the air ; Varuna, the water ; the Sun ; the Moon; and other elementary and planetary personages. It is a domestic worship, adapted rather for use in households than in temples.

The Vedas are supposed to have been compiled about 1300 or 1500 B.C., and may thus be reckoned among the most venerable of human liturgies. The allusions in the hymns show them to have been the work of a race busied with tillage, and flocks, and herds, and acquainted with horses, chariots, caparisons, the forging of iron armour, and weaving : a fair-skinned race among darker populations ; a race that had its origin west and north of the Indus —the Aryan race, the fathers of all modern civilisation.

It may be interesting, while on this subject, to subjoin two striking extracts from Professor WILSON's translation of the Vedas. " O Agni ! when thou hast yoked thy bright-red horses, swift as

P

the wind to thy car, thy roar is like a bull's, and thou enwrappest the forest trees with a banner of smoke! Let us not, O Agni, suffer injury through thy friendship."

"I declare the valorous deeds of old of Indra, which the Thunderer has achieved! He clove the cloud! He cast the waters down to earth! He broke the way for the torrents of the mountain!"

621. According to the tenets of Buddhism, there are *three doors* by which sin may be committed—the body, the mouth, and the mind; that is to say, by thought, or word, or deed.

ELEVENTH PART.

632. On great festivals, it is customary to caparison the procession elephants with face-cloths and the other paraphernalia named in the text. With the torches and cressets flaming round the huge beasts at night, the effect is very striking, as they go on their stately march, followed by crowds of people, through the streets of the town.

636. "Sun-descended King," literally Head of the Solar Dynasty, *Suriyavansa*, from which many of the ancient kings of the East fabled themselves sprung. See the note to the fourth stanza, p. 198, *supra*.

638. This eight-curved gem is frequently mentioned in other Buddhistic legends, for instance, the *Ummagga Jātakē*.

TWELFTH PART.

654. The pouring of water on newly-married people is an ancient marriage ceremony among the Sinhalese,

The exclamation "AYIBŌWAN!"—"May your Life be Long!" is the respectful form of salutation among the Sinhalese to this day.

658. BRAHASPATI is, according to Hindu mythology, the regent of the planet Jupiter, and the *guru* or teacher of the gods. He presides over Thursday. The mango-tree is sacred to him.

661. As before noted, a white horse is held in great estimation among Eastern nations. So, too, a white elephant.

THIRTEENTH PART.

664. Peacocks, which abound wild in Ceylon forests, and in Hambantota district especially, announce the coming of a storm by loud screaming and flapping of wings. See also the forty-seventh stanza.

677. This allusion to the maintenance of ancient usages was probably in compliment to the doings of King WIMALA DHARMA, who had, shortly before the date of the poem, restored the Buddhist religion, and revived ancient customs and ceremonies.

679. *The Four Great Truths* Buddhism teaches are—
1. Sorrow is connected with life in every state :
2. Men cling to life on account of their passions and desires :
3. The means conducive to the complete subjugation of the passions :
4. The state preparatory to the attainment of NIRVĀNA, in which the passions are overcome, and all desire for further life annihilated.

These are summed up by SCHLAGINTWEIT (*Buddhism in Tibet*, p. 16) as—

THE PAIN : THE PRODUCTION : THE CESSATION : THE PATH.

In detailing, he continues, the moral precepts of the fourth truth, the attainment of NIRVĀNA, eight good paths are enumerated :—
1. The right opinion, or orthodoxy.
2. The right judgment, which dispels all doubt.
3. The right words, or perfect meditation.
4. The right conduct, or keeping always in view a pure and honest aim.
5. The right livelihood, or subsistence by a sinless occupation.
6. The rightly directed understanding which leads to final emancipation ("to the other side of the river ").
7. The right memory.
8. The right meditation, or tranquil mind, by which perfect and imperturbable mental calm may be obtained.

The attainment of perfect calm is always held out, wisely enough, as an object most desirable. *In perfect quiescence,* say Buddhists, *lies the highest form of enjoyment!* It is not a doctrine adapted to stirring Anglo-Saxon ideas and impulses, though, in a qualified degree, it may once, perhaps, have been suited to the inhabitants of a sunny tropical island that realised Tennyson's exquisite description:

——"island at the gateways of the day !
Larger constellations burning, mellow moons and happy skies,
Breadths of tropic shade and palms in cluster—knots of Paradise!
Never comes the trader, never floats an European flag;
Slides the bird o'er lustrous moorland, swings the trailer from the crag !
Droops the heavy-blossomed bower, hangs the heavy-fruited tree ;
Summer isle of Eden, lying in dark purple spheres of sea !
There, methinks, would be enjoyment more than in this march of mind,
In the steamship, in the railway, in the thoughts that shake mankind "

Fortunately, now-a-days, CEYLON, while as nobly gifted as ever in the rare beauty the poet sings, is not without her due share of progress, moral and material. The axe rings in her forests, and flourishing domains take the place of pathless jungles : rivers are bridged, and roads permeate through the length and breadth of the land : her towns and country-places abound with evidence of well-directed energy, and wide diffusion of wealth and comfort : steamers and other shipping crowd her harbours : locomotives speed through her sylvan valleys and fastnesses : irrigation works are carried steadily forward : and, what is better than all, peace is within her borders : want and distress are rare : the schools are thronged with scholars : and her people, consisting of so many widely diverse creeds and nationalities, combine to present the cheering spectacle of a community distinguished for genuine well-doing, self-respect, loyalty and order. ESTO PERPETUA !

680. *Sovān*, the first of the four stages or paths leading to NIRVĀNA.

NIRVĀNA is the highest attainable felicity, wherein the passions are entirely destroyed, animal functions cease, the principle of life is extinguished, the soul and sentient faculties are emancipated from further transmigration. It is hard to grasp at a definite idea of what the term fully and really implies.

Colonel FORBES's remarks (*Eleven Years in Ceylon*) on this head deserve notice. It is, he considers, uncertain if we have just equivalents in English [which is perfectly true], or the Buddhists in their vernacular languages, for the subtle expression NIRVĀNA, which may have been intended to remain a mystery of Buddhistic doctrine. From a comparison of the many different epithets used as synonymous with or illustrative of it, there is reason to believe the phrase "having attained NIRVĀNA," signifies not only that the spirit, from that time forth, is emancipated from the body, but, having been gradually and finally purified, remains at last untroubled by any passion or aspiration ; it is, then and for ever, an essence of purity and virtue !

Although the final goal at which it aims would appear to be of so negative a character, Buddhism, as MAX MÜLLER has eloquently shown, taught a practical morality of the highest and purest kind. Besides the five great commands—which prohibit the taking of life, theft, adultery, lying, and drunkenness—every shade of vice and hypocrisy, anger, pride, suspicion, greediness, gossiping, cruelty to animals, is guarded against by special precepts. Among the virtues recommended are reverence for parents, care of children, submission to authority, gratitude, moderation in prosperity, resignation in trial, equanimity at all times, the duty of forgiving insults, and *not rewarding evil for evil*. *Maitri*, from which, we are told, all virtues proceed, BURNOUF says should be translated by *charity*. " It (Maitri) does not express friendship, or the feeling of particular affection a man has for one or more of his fellow-creatures ; but that universal feeling which inspires us with goodwill towards all men, and constant willingness to help them."

But though it seems generally agreed that the moral code of Buddha, " for pureness, excellence, and wisdom would appear to be second only to that of the Divine Lawgiver," the weakness and the experience of every thinking man convincingly teach him that out of no such theoretical code, however pure, is the right way of living to be learned; and that the truest and the best source of goodness and happiness is found in Christianity alone.

681. The proper names in this and the following stanzas demand notice, which will best be accorded by giving a brief summary of the main incidents of the Great Teacher's life in what his followers call his last birth before becoming BUDDHA.

He was born probably in the sixth century before the Christian era, as PRINCE SAKYAMUNI or SIDDHARTA, the son of King SUDDHO-

DENA (of the clan of the GAUTAMAS,) who reigned at Kapilavastu, in Gorukpur, somewhere on the confines of Oude and Nepal. MÁYA was the queen of SUDDHODENA, and mother of the Bōdisat. There is, it has been remarked, much resemblance between the legends told of her and those of the VIRGIN MARY. On the same day with SAKYAMUNI were born YASŌDARA (daughter of DANDAPANI, King of Koli), whom he afterwards married in his seventeenth year ; and ANANDA, who, after the Prince became BUDDHA, accompanied him as a pupil and friend. It was ANANDA who subsequently compiled the first portion of the *Tripitaka* (The Three Baskets), the *Sútras*, or discourses of BUDDHA. The queen, YASŌDARA, bore her husband a son, RAHULA, who was afterwards ordained a priest by his father.

At thirty the Prince resolved on becoming an ascetic, or religious mendicant. He abandoned all secular ties ; and after undergoing fierce temptation from the demons, and subjecting himself to a life of penance and asceticism for six years, he attained, as he believed, the true knowledge which discloses the cause and destroys the fear of all the changes inherent in life. Thenceforward he assumed the name of BUDDHA, the All-Wise or the Enlightened. He proceeded to Benares, and from that time spent the remainder of his life, upwards of forty years, in teaching and preaching his gospel of emancipation from suffering and sin. At Srasvati (Buddha Gaya), at Benares, at Rajagaha, and Vaisali, he abode and taught. At Srasvati, the capital of Kosala, a wealthy merchant, ANATHA-PINDADA, called in the legend, ANĒPIDU, built him and his disciples a sumptuous vihāra. The King of Kosala became a convert. After twelve years' absence, BUDDHA visited his father at Kapilavastu, on which occasion it is alleged he performed many miracles, and converted all the Sakyas (the tribe to which his own family belonged) to the Faith. His wife and his aunt became his followers. It is said he travelled over a wide extent of country, and even visited Ceylon. He died when over eighty years of age, under a Bō-tree at Kusināra. After his death, his body was burnt, and his relics being distributed, dome-shaped dāgobas or monumental relic-crypts were erected to contain them. These are plentiful all over Ceylon.

As in the early Christian Church, so in the Buddhistic, several Great Councils are recorded to have been held—one immediately after BUDDHA's death, a second about a hundred years later, a third about 240 B.C. From the Founder's days, the clergy had lived apart from the laity in vihāras (monasteries); and the Councils appear to have been held to settle matters of doctrine and clerical discipline, and to extend the faith in foreign parts. It spread, too, and still prevails in China, Japan, Siam, Burmah, Tibet, Kashmir, and Ceylon. The Mongols of Central Asia cherish it as their form of religious belief; and it is said to have a footing in Siberia, and even in Swedish Lapland. It was once dominant in India Proper, but it rapidly fell into decay there, and all traces of it as a living faith disappeared, except among non-Hindu races at the foot of the Himalayan chain.—(See article *Buddhism*, CHAMBERS'S *Information for the People*, and MAX MÜLLER'S·Essays on *Comparative Mythology*.)

A place may be found here for M. BARTHÉLEMY SAINT-HILAIRE'S eloquent words on the teaching of BUDDHA : Je n'hésite pas à ajouter que, sauf le CHRIST tout seul, il n'est point, parmi les fondateurs de religion, de figure plus pure ni plus touchante que celle de Bouddha. Sa vie n'a point de tâche. Son constant héroisme égale sa conviction ; et si la théorie qu'il préconise est fausse, les exemples personnels qu'il donne sont irréprochables. Il est le modèle achevé de toutes les vertus qu'il prêche : son abnégation, sa charité, son inaltérable douceur, ne se démentent point un seul instant : il abandonne à vingt-neuf ans la cour du roi son père pour se faire religieux et mendiant : il prépare silencieusement sa doctrine par six années de retraite et de méditation : il la propage par la seule puissance de la parole et de la persuasion, pendant plus d'un demi-siècle : et quand il meurt entre les bras de ses disciples, c'est avec la sérénité d'un sage qui a pratiqué le bien toute sa vie, et qui est assuré d'avoir trouvé le vrai.—(*Le Bouddha et sa Religion.*)

687. *The Saka Era*, one commonly employed in ancient Sinhalese literature, and still in use in calculating horoscopes, is said to date from the time of King SAKA. It commences seventy-eight years after the Christian Era. Hence 1532 would correspond with 1610, A.D., which is, accordingly, the date of the poem. The era of BUDDHA dates from 543 B.C., the year of the Teacher's death, twenty-three centuries ago.

BUDDHISTIC AND OTHER REMAINS IN HAMBANTOTA DISTRICT.

While on the subject of Buddhism, an extract from some notes on ancient Buddhistic and other remains, and existing conventual establishments, to be found in the district (Hambantota), of which the writer has administrative charge, may not be out of place. The district is in the south-east of Ceylon, and has about a hundred miles of sea-board, stretching to a considerable distance inland. Everywhere are to be found traces in plenty of the ancient occupation of the country, which, as a separate principality, under the name of *Maha Ruhuna*, having its capital at Mágama, now an insignificant hamlet, attained, more than two thousand years ago, great splendour and prosperity, so much so as to have its chief city known to the geographers of the West. So thickly peopled was the realm, says local tradition, with a noble hyperbole utterly regardless of probability, that a squirrel could travel from house-top to house-top without ever touching the ground, from Mágama to Anurádhapura in the north of the island! That ancient myth, which appears in the romantic legends of many nations, of a princess, or other dame of high degree, abandoned in a boat or raft, and drifted at the mercy of the wind and waves, until she is borne in safety to a far-away shore, where a king is waiting to welcome and wed her, and, of course, "live happy ever afterwards," is localised here at Duráva, about twenty miles from Hambantota. From the rocks at Duráva have been hewn, as marks remaining abundantly show, the huge granite blocks, monoliths sometimes more than thirty feet long and eight in girth, used in building the palace and temples at Tissamaharáma, nine miles inland. At Kirinda, near Duráva, are many fantastically shaped rocks piled round each other in grotesque confusion, on one of which is an inscription, having at one side the royal device of the sun and moon. Near this are the remains of an old dágoba, said to have been built as a thank-offering for the safe voyage of the Princess. Ancient inscriptions carved on granite rocks are to be met with in great plenty all over the district, as at Vádigala, between Tangalla and Hambantota, Angulakolawala, and Mulgirigala.

Mulgirigala is one of the most flourishing and picturesque Buddhist monasteries in the province, and is kept in admirable order. The priests are extremely courteous to travellers, for whose reception a hall has been built. Mention is made of the place in

Sinhalese chronicles so early as 120 B.C.—an antiquity to which, it need hardly be said, no monastic establishment in the West can lay claim.

The view in the early morning from the lofty rock on which the dāgoba stands is very beautiful. On the shoulder of the rock is the cave, converted into a temple, now filled with figures of Buddha in various attitudes. The lands belonging to the monastery are of considerable extent and value.

About six miles off, across country, stands Kahagalwihāra, originally founded seventeen hundred years ago. Here too is an inscription on the rock where the dāgoba is built, and many remains of great interest are scattered about. As at Mulgirigala, a comfortable reception-hall is at the service of the traveller, being in fact the hall where *bana* is read—the preaching hall of the monastery. This wihára has many affiliated temples, or, so to speak, chapelries, in various parts of the district; and the appointment of priests to serve in them, as they become vacant, rests with the Prior at the monastery, assisted, when necessary, by a council of other priests. Properly speaking, the council should consist of ten, but five constitute a quorum. The council regulates matters ecclesiastical as pertaining to the monastery and its dependencies. The former Prior died in March 1869, and his remains were burnt with the usual ceremonies. On his decease, according to the established rule now in force, the senior of his pupils succeeded to the priorate. The dependent temples are thirteen in number, and the priests attached to them twenty-eight. Here, as in many other respects, may be noted—what has often excited remark in other countries where Buddhism prevails—how many points of resemblance exist between the ceremonies, discipline, and administration of Buddhist wiháras and those of monastic institutions of mediæval times in Europe. To quote the author of the *History of Architecture,* "Any one who has seen Buddhist priests celebrate matins or vespers, or their more pompous ceremonies, will have no difficulty in understanding the uses of every part of the magnificent edifices now in ruins in many parts of India. To those who have not witnessed these ceremonies, it will suffice to say, that in the principal forms they resemble the Roman Catholics. This has attracted the attention of every Roman Catholic priest or missionary who has visited Buddhist countries, from the earliest missions to China to the most recent journey into Tibet of Messrs Huc and

Gabet. All the latter can suggest by way of explanation is *Que le diable y'est pour beaucoup!*"

It is, however, at and in the neighbourhood of Tihawa, or Tissamaharáma, about twenty miles from Hambantota, that the grandest memorials of the olden time are to be seen. Though the country between Tihawa and the sea is now a desolate wilderness, there can be no doubt tradition speaks truly when it alleges the whole was at one time densely peopled and highly cultivated, the magnificent reservoir of Tihawa supplying the whole tract. The tank was itself fed by a channel four miles in length, conveying water from the amuna, or anicut of masonry, thrown across the Mágam River at Mayilagastota. The soil is a rich black loam, certain, were water again forthcoming, to be as productive as it was of old. I rejoice to think that there is now (1871) a near prospect of a partial restoration of this great irrigation work, destined to "scatter plenty o'er a smiling land," and to transform, by a magic of the most beneficent sort, a trackless jungle into the granary and garden of the south of Ceylon.

Everywhere along the track leading from Kirinda to Tissamaha-ráma, if the ground be slightly scratched, ashes will be found—traces as suggestive of ancient human habitations as are the kitchen-middens that have of late years caused so much stir in Europe. Here and there, in what is now a thorny brake, are places where, if old legends may be trusted, kings and queens went, twenty centuries ago, a-pleasuring in golden chariots drawn by gaily caparisoned horses; and thickets overgrown with weeds and underwood, the haunt of the elephant, bear, and leopard, occupy the site of royal pavilions, where of old was held high festival with revelry and song!

Around Tihawa, the ground, when dug up, is found thickly strewn with bricks innumerable, hard, well burnt, and of a large size. The traveller, as he approaches the Great Dágoba sees group after group of upright granite blocks, ranged in lines, and recalling, at the first glance, the Druidical remains met with in Western Europe. The blocks have been wedged out of the rocks on the sea-shore, nine miles off, and are mostly unwrought otherwise. Some are eight feet in girth and stand twenty to thirty feet above the ground; and it may be assumed that one-third more is underground. These groups are to be found in all directions round, and sometimes at great distances from the Great Dágoba. How they were taken there and upraised is a marvel, unless we credit the ancient inhabitants with a knowledge of mechanical appliances almost on a par with those in use in modern days. One is irresistibly reminded of the answer to Horace Smith's spirited "Address to the Egyptian Mummy"—

—————" Men of yore
Were versed in all the science you can mention !
Who hath not heard of Egypt's peerless lore,
Her patient skill, acuteness of invention ?
Although her mighty toils unearthly seem,
Those blocks were brought on railroads and by steam !"

It would be going too far to assert as much as this; nor does the theory held by the inhabitants offer a very satisfactory solution. They maintain that the blocks were moved by giants—there having been Anakim in the land of old—of the measure of whose strength an idea may be formed when we are told that one of them with his right hand compressed the head of the king's chief elephant, and thus shaped the two huge hollows now to be seen at the temples of all animals of that species ! Many legends continue to float about these out-of-the-way places, some extravagant enough, others undoubtedly founded on fact. Sometimes these stories recount the benefits conferred on the country by well-planned schemes of irrigation and tillage, sometimes they celebrate the liberal grants to ecclesiastics, and the enormous fabrics raised in honour of the Faith, by which, as did good King DAVID of Scotland, at Melrose and elsewhere, the monarchs of Ceylon proved themselves to be "sair saints for the Crown ! "

At Tissamaharáma are four dágobas, all originally dome-shaped. They are, respectively, the Great Dágoba, Sandhagiri, Yata-ala, and the Gem Dágoba. The three last named are easily climbed. On Yata-ala, on the occasion of one of my visits, I found some wild elephants, which abound in the jungles round about, had, with the well-known curiosity of their species, made their way to the top a few days before. The dágobas have been built throughout of brick, many of which have peculiar masonic marks on them traced before burning. Similar marks I have found on bricks at Kataragama, Kahagalwihára, and elsewhere.

In many of the mediæval abbeys and priories in Britain,* peculiar marks are to be found on the masonry, such marks varying in different buildings. The supposition regarding them is that they were the secret marks of the *Freemasons* by whom these noble piles

* Lanercost in Cumberland is a case in point.

were reared, and who, formed into guilds or companies, travelled from place to place as their services were required. They, as distinguished from inferior craftsmen, mostly in those days villeins of the soil, *adscripti glebœ*, were free, and so styled themselves. It is from them—and they should rather be called artists than craftsmen, so grand were their achievements, and so penetrated with a sense of the true and beautiful, and of elevated religious feeling—it is from their guilds that the *Freemasons* of the present day derive their honourable origin and constitution. To revert, however, to the subject in hand—it may perhaps not be unreasonable to think that the secret marks on the bricks may reveal some ancient confraternity of the same sort.

A dāgoba, as its name implies, is a receptacle for relics ; and in the centre of each is to be found a hollow, containing what an ancient faith held precious. At Yata-ala this is well-shown, an entrance a yard wide leading to the heart of the building. It was above this hollow crypt—the receptacle for relics—that the piety of ancient days led men to build a lofty pile, either of the shape of a pyramid, as in Egypt, or of a dome, as in the dāgobas of Ceylon ; a landmark visible from afar in a level country, and showing travellers and pilgrims at a great distance where the objects held in reverence by them lay enshrined. It is curious to reflect that to this feeling, appreciatively adopted by Christianity from paganism, we owe the magnificent domes of Constantinople, of Rome, and our own St Paul's.

All the dāgobas were, no doubt, originally faced with well-cemented bricks, and plastered and otherwise embellished, having probably finials at the top of gold or other precious material. The outer facing has long ago disappeared ; but in the case of the Great Dāgoba, a great part, to the height of a hundred feet above the ground, has been recently renewed. This is solely owing to the exertions of a Buddhist priest, SOMANA IRA UNNĀNSÉ, who settled here about fifteen years ago, and has devoted himself to the task of improving the place and obtaining alms for the repair of the fabric. Bricks are readily to be had by digging anywhere round about. The lime is brought from fifty to sixty miles off. It is no small triumph for the priest that so much has been achieved. He spends most of his time in travelling through Ceylon soliciting contributions in aid of his colossal work. He has put up buildings for devotees and pilgrims who visit the dāgobas, and very comfortable quarters for his coolies and for the settlers who have accompanied him, and an excellent unfurnished bungalow, literally in "a garden of cucumbers," for the reception of English travellers, whom he welcomes with great cordiality to the spot. I do not doubt, if this enthusiastic man's life is spared, the whole of the work he has set his heart upon will be completed. When, in addition to this, the Irrigation Works are perfected, his measure of satisfaction will be full.

At the base of the Great Dāgoba have originally been four large shrines. The massive stone tables for oblations still remain ; and here to this day offerings of flowers, and at nights of little earthenware cups of oil with lighted wicks, are duly made. It serves to recall the Latin epitaph—

> "Sit tibi terra levis !
> *Quisquis huic tumulo*
> *Posuit ardentem lucernam,*
> Illius cineres
> Aurea terra tegat !"

Only one figure, and that mutilated, of Buddha is now to be seen. It is of dolomite. In the writer's possession is a very ancient figure of Buddha in lead, about four inches in height, mounted on a sort of pedestal also of lead. This was found in the jungle near Tihawa. The figure is sitting cross-legged under a Bo-tree, and is very ancient.

Around the four shrines was anciently much ornamental work, part still remaining, among which are conspicuous elephants' heads spiritedly executed in dolomite. Along the circular way, still easily traceable between the base of the dome and the outer precinct, past the colossal statues of the Great Reformer—then, as are the figures of Buddha always, the very embodiment of mildness, immobility, and calm—and thence by the broad avenue to Sandhagiri Dāgoba at the distance of a few furlongs, went, no doubt, some twenty centuries ago, at the stated periods, with flashing torches and clash of cymbals and clamour of shrilly fifes, many a stately procession of priest and king, and worshippers of high and low degree. In sight of the magnificent structures still remaining, it needs but little force of imagination to people the place with visions of the past !

The jungle for miles round abounds with ruins. Near the site of the palace described in the next paragraph is an octagonal granite block, ten feet in girth, and eight high, bearing an inscription in Nagari. This block is, according to tradition, the post to which

the royal Tusker Elephant was tied. Marks on one of the faces
are pointed out as having been worn by his chains. Within forty
paces is the grandest group of all the monoliths, occupying the site
of the ancient palace, on a gentle slope between the Gem Dāgoba
and Yata-ala. The blocks are seventy in number, in ten rows of
seven each, standing thirty feet above the ground, seven feet in
girth, and having the tops chiselled to hold massive wooden beams.
Probably the lower portion was an open Hall of Audience, while
the royal pavilion was of timber at the top of the columns. The
surrounding country between the palace and the river is undulat-
ing, and if the dense jungle were cleared, and only the large timber
which flourishes here were left standing, would be park-like and
extremely picturesque. According to tradition, the kings did not
permanently live here, but at Māgama ; and there is reason to
think, from the appearance of the environs of Tissamaharáma, that
the so-called palace was of the nature of a lodge in the midst of a
royal pleasance, such as Eastern kings have always affected for
purposes of sport and recreation. The old Persian kings had, each
of them, his παράδεισος : and Sinhalese literature, as the *Kusa
Játaké* abundantly shows, teems with allusions to the royal plea-
sure-grounds. Tihawa was one in remote ages—but the times are
changed !

> " It was a gallant spot in days of yore !
> But something ails it *now :* the place is curst ! "

A spectator standing on the top of the Great Dāgoba, or of
Sandhagiri, and looking towards what was once the palace and
pleasance, the silver streak of sea, and the quick-flowing river,
itself perpetually beautiful, and attempting to picture to himself
the place as it may have appeared two thousand years ago, is
reminded of the pregnant passage in *Purchas's Pilgrimage*—" *Here
the Khan Kubla commanded a palace to be built, and a stately garden
thereunto : and thus ten miles of fertile ground were enclosed ;* " and
of Coleridge's wonderful poem, built up in a dream, on that text :

> " In Xanadu did Kubla Khan
>   A stately pleasure dome decree,
> Where Alph, the sacred river, ran
> Through caverns measureless to man,
>   Down to a sunless sea !
> So twice five miles of fertile ground,
> With walls and towers were girdled round :

And there were gardens bright with sinuous rills,
Where blossomed many an incense-bearing tree:
And here were forests ancient as the hills,
Enfolding sunny spots of greenery!"

Across the river, about two miles from the Great Dāgoba, are two very remarkable natural anicuts of rock, called Mahagalamuna and Kudagalamuna. It is highly probable they first gave the idea to the ancient inhabitants of the anicut of masonry constructed higher up at Mayilagastota, to which were owing the productiveness and renown of the district. Besides the attraction which the fertility of the country would offer to the earliest settlers, however, it cannot be doubted that the place had in their eyes another and especial advantage, in the nearness of the salt-lagoons, then, as now, of inestimable value to the State. In these lagoons abundant salt of the finest quality forms naturally, without involving any labour or outlay beyond the trouble of gathering, and, at the present day, enables the Ceylon Government to supply at a very trifling cost this essential article of diet. One of the lagoons, close to Hambantota, the Maha Lewāya, a shallow pond about a mile in diameter, has yielded for many years, and year after year, salt worth on an average about eight thousand pounds annually, and may thus be looked upon as the most valuable Crown domain in Ceylon. The other lagoons are also, as a general rule, fairly productive.

Englishmen, accustomed to abundance of the best salt at a trifling price, and residents in Ceylon at present, when excellent salt is readily to be had everywhere, can scarcely realise how important the nearness of the salt-lagoons must have been considered in ancient days. In the earlier part of the present century, when the last Kandyan King was at war with England, and, traffic being at an end, only such salt as could be smuggled across the frontier found its way to his dominions, the sufferings undergone for want of it were extreme. How high a value is set upon salt by the people may be illustrated by what occurred in the Southern Province, within the writer's recollection, some twelve or thirteen years ago. An absurd and utterly groundless rumour was spread abroad among the villagers that a foreign man-of-war was about to bombard Galle, and do unheard-of havoc in the country round about. Upon this, some of the villagers abandoned their homes, and, taking with them an *ample supply of salt, and little else*, fled into the jungle, whence they duly emerged a few days afterwards, and were much laughed at for their pains !

To revert to the subject of Buddhist remains. About thirty-four miles from Hambantota, on the top of what is now an inaccessible rock, are the ruins of the Akāsēchayityawihāra, or *the temple in the sky*. This is unapproachable without staging and ladders.* It is visible from a great distance, and is strikingly picturesque. But all over the district, not only in Māgam, but in Giruva Pattu, dāgobas are to be seen perched on the top of granitic rocks, rising sheer from the plain. The whole district offers a promising field to any student of Buddhistic architecture and polity.

* It was last climbed in this way, a few years ago, by Mr L. Ludovici, for purposes connected with the general survey of the Island. Mr Ludovici, it may be added, is understood to be about to publish a Descriptive Gazetteer of Ceylon, a much needed work, which cannot fail to be of great géneral interest and usefulness.

[On the subject of the removal of large monoliths, the subjoined extract from Max Müller's able paper on *Cornish Antiquities* deserves especial attention : " Marvellous as are the remains of that primitive style of architectural art, the only real problem they offer is how such large stones could have been brought together from a distance, and how such enormous weights could have been lifted up. The first question is answered by ropes and rollers : and the mural sculptures of Nineveh show us what can be done by such simple machinery. We there see the whole picture of how these colossal blocks of stone were moved from the quarry to the place where they were wanted. Given plenty of time, and plenty of men and oxen, and there is no block that could not be brought to its right place by means of ropes and rollers. And that our forefathers did not stint themselves either in time or in men, or other cattle, when engaged in erecting such monuments, we know even from comparatively recent times."]

Sinhalese Epigrams and Stories.

THE *Pratyasataka*, or Century of Maxims, from which the subjoined epigrams are taken, is a compilation from different writers. When, or by whom, this anthology was compiled is not known. It bears evidence of borrowing from the *Hitopadesa*.

DOCTOR AND PATIENT.

When a patient falls sick, and is seriously ill,
He looks on the doctor, who gives him a pill
Or a potion, as INDRA, the god of the sky!
This is while the invalid fears he may die!
But, as he recovers, the doctor appears
A mere man! Then, when rid of his fears,
A devil! And last, when he's fully restored,
The doctor's a beggar, contemned and abhorred!

AN IMPOSSIBLE CONVERSION.

With nine rare gems bedeck the crow:
Around his neck let sapphires glow:
Gild all his plumes!—This truth is clear,
A swan he never will appear!

SELF-INTEREST.

The birds the barren tree forsake:
The beasts desert the withered brake:
Bees quit the flower's unhoneyed cup:
Dry twigs no moisture may drink up:

Q

No caterers for the poor make sport :
Few lords frequent a tyrant's court—
Self-seekers all !   In every race
Our interest holds the foremost place !

A BUDDHISTIC DOGMA.

Not from the king that rules the realm proceed our ills and
    woes,
Nor from the ministers of state, our kinsmen, or our foes !
Nor from the shining host of orbs that glitter in the sky,
Descend the ills that compass us, and shall do till we die,
And after !   But the real source of all our woes on earth,
Is merit or demerit earned within a previous birth !*

WHAT THINGS GIVE JOY?

What things give joy ?   To men benumbed
    The pleasing warmth of day ;
The blithesome prattle of a child
    That revels in its play ;
And gifts from royal hands are sweet ;
    And sweet a landscape fair :
These things give gladness to the heart,
    Dispelling grief and care.

TRUE LEARNING.

True learning is a treasure no king can take away ;
No thieves that store may pilfer—no man its worth gainsay !
Light is its load in travel, not burdensome the least;
The more 'tis shared with others, the more it is increased !
Of all the crowd of mortals, this truth will stand confessed,
The learned man ranks ever pre-eminent and best !

PURITY.

Where shall purity be found ?
In the feet that print the ground
Bound on works of grace and merit;

* See p. 220, *supra.*

In the mercy-loving spirit ;
In the hands that succour well
Helpless folk ; in lips that dwell
Lovingly on what of yore
BUDDHA taught us to adore !

WISDOM.

Wisdom giveth grace to men
   Unbeautiful ! It is a treasure
Never failing; and again
   'Tis a friend that yields us pleasure,
Wealth, and boons, and high renown !
   In a far and foreign nation
'Tis a kinsman that doth own
   Love and kinship : it hath station,
Worthy of the first regard :
   'Tis a duty all should cherish :—
He that is of it debarred
   Is but as the beasts that perish !

DOMESTIC MISFORTUNES.

Living in a place of strife,
Mated with a low-born wife,
Eating bad, unwholesome diet,
Troubled by a dame unquiet,
Owning children spoilt and wild,
Daughters widowed or beguiled—
Unto whomsoe'er they fall,
These are sore misfortunes all !

MEDIO TUTISSIMUS IBIS !

If all too intimate you grow
   With fire, the King, or damsel fair,
'Tis parlous thing—it worketh woe :
   For ruin soon may be your share !
And yet, if utterly you shun
   All three, *that* also tends to shame :

So take a middle course, the one
  To hold you free from scathe and blame !

GOOD FORTUNE.

Out of mud the lotus springs :
Clay yields gold and precious things :
Oysters pearls : bright silks the worm—
Fit to robe the daintiest form !
From the bull the bezoar good,
Musk from deer, and flame from wood,
Come : and honey sweet and bland
From the jungly desert land.
Sources thus of little worth
Yield the precious things of earth :
So, if once upon a child
Happy Fortune shall have smiled,
Lofty birth or noble kin
Needs he none ! *He* still will win !

THE HUSBAND'S REMEDY.

If a wife for ever quarrels
  With her lord, and disobeys;
If, indifferent in her morals,
  She declines to mend her ways;
If too fond or foul of others
  She should fall—or eat too much ;
If she gads about, and bothers :
  When a woman's ways are such,
Though twice five her children be,
Seek the means of getting free !
Try the fit and proper course,
Nought will answer but DIVORCE !

THE IGNORANT MAN.

The owl sees nought at noonday bright :
The crow sees nothing in the night :
The man untaught is worse than they ;
For *he* sees nought by night or day !

NO ONE IS CONTENT.

Though more and more his riches grow,
  The King withal content is never !
Insatiate is the sea, although
  Down to his shore flows every river !
Eager and restless still the eye
  On beauteous sights unsated gazes !
Untired the wise love converse high,
  On it bestowing endless praises !

THE MIGHT OF MERCY.

Take mercy and forbearance,
  So armèd meet the foe !
The wicked cannot harm thee :
  Innocuous falls the blow !
The fire for want of fuel
  To nothingness is brought :
And mercy and forbearance
  Bring violence to nought !

MAKING A VIRTUE OF NECESSITY—AND ITS REWARD.

The feeble oft are seen
  Religious and devout ;
The dames of ugly mien
  Are chaste beyond a doubt ;
The foolish best demean
  Themselves by saying nought !
So act these folk because
  None other may they dare,
And yet the world's applause
  Falls often to their share !

THE PEACEFUL FLOURISH.

Three cubs the lioness brings forth,
  The tiger's young are five,

The cow's but one—and yet on earth
Meek cattle live and thrive,
While few the savage beasts of prey!
With men the same we see :
The fierce and grasping soon decay,
The peaceful flourish free!

MATCHMAKING.

When daughters grow up and are thinking of marriage,
Their mothers will all but rich husbands disparage ;
To worth and good sense have few fathers objections ;
The kinsfolk look mostly to birth and connections;
But the damsels themselves, with their hearts for their tutors,
Think gay, handsome lovers the dearest of·suitors !

THREE JEWELS.

The sun above the sky is a jewel rich and rare :
Within our homes a child is a gem beyond compare :
And a jewel is the wise in the thronged assembly hall :
As shining gems are these and precious are they all!

LOW SOCIETY.

Better to haunt the desert brake,
Where savage beasts their refuge take,
To feed on herbs, in foliage dressed,
To use the grass as couch of rest—
Better 'tis thus to dwell serene,
Than herd with comrades base and mean !

Sinhalese Stories.

HOW TO RESTORE SPEECH TO THE DUMB.

IF a dispute is going on, a woman, even if she is dumb, will find her tongue to take part in it! What is more, she often gets the best of it.

Long ago, a King—or, as some say, a very wealthy man, but it does not matter which, though a King sounds better—had an only child, a daughter, the heiress of all his wealth, who could not, or would not speak. He tried all means to cure her, but in vain. At last he sent forth a proclamation that whoever, being of fitting degree, could restore speech to his daughter, should marry her and eventually be lord of all her father's wealth. Many tried, but all failed. At last a Prince who had a magical gift, that of causing things inanimate to talk with him, came forward and was admitted to the hall where the Princess was. He spoke to her, and tried to induce her to speak, but answer he got none!

Now, a lamp was hanging in the hall, and to it the Prince good-humouredly addressed himself. "Lamp," said he, "I will tell you a story." "Say on," replied the lamp. "Well," went on the Prince, "four travellers—a Carpenter, a Painter, a Cloth Merchant, and a Jeweller—set out on a journey. By and by they came to a resthouse, halted there, and prepared their food. The keeper of the resthouse had laid on the floor a log of wood very suitable for carving. The Carpenter seeing this, pulled out his carving gear and carved the log into the shape of a woman, life size, and exquisitely beautiful. The Painter next took his brushes and colours, and painted the figure till it shone as brilliantly fair as a goddess. Then the Cloth Merchant opened his packages, chose the finest silks and embroidered robes, and dressed the figure in his choicest bravery. The Jeweller took gems, earrings, necklaces, and bangles, and all such things, and bedecked the figure with them. Last of all, the figure was endowed with life. I do not take on me to explain how that came about, but it was the fact!" "No more do I," said the lamp, "but pray go on. I hate digressions!" "When," continued the Prince, "that exquisitely beautiful being burst into life, all the four fell violently in love with her, and each wished to make her his wife. 'Why, I shaped that matchless figure,' said the Carpenter. 'And I bestowed on her that blooming complexion,' retorted the Painter, 'And I robed her,' exclaimed the Merchant. 'But what are your choicest robes to the costly gems which were my gift? A woman is of little account without jewels!' cried the Jeweller. Thus they went on clamouring and disputing. Now, O lamp! who was to be declared the rightful owner?"

First the lamp said one and then another, giving reasons—and whatever the lamp said the Prince contradicted. The dispute waxed hot and furious, but seemed never to come nearer to an end.

The Princess heard all the dispute, and held her peace a long time. At last she could bear to keep silent no longer. So she cried, "You are both silly! The true owner was none of the four, but the keeper of the resthouse, for to him the wood she was made of belonged!" "By my two eyes," said the Prince, "you are in the right, O my Princess! And now that you have spoken, let me claim my reward and take you for my wife!" So they went before the King, who was enchanted with the cure; and they were married straightway and lived happy ever afterwards—at least it is said the Princess never gave her husband any cause after marriage to reproach her for too persistently holding her peace!

THE PANDIT AND THE SHE-FIEND.

There are beings in great numbers called fiends. They are of both sexes. The he-fiend is called *Yakā*, the she-fiend *Yakinni*. They often appear on the earth. They may, if they like, benefit by BUDDHA's teaching, and attain *Nirvāna*. You may know Yakās, if you meet them, by the redness of their eyes, which do not twinkle as do the eyes of men.

Once upon a time a poor woman went to a tank to bathe her child. She bathed and dressed the child, set him on the bund to play, and then went into the water herself to bathe. While there, a *Yakinni*, to all appearance a woman of the same class as the one bathing, came up and felt a great desire to carry off the child and eat him up, as he was plump. You must know that fiends are cannibals. Indeed, they have no scruples, and will eat almost anything. They often open graves to feast on the dead. Feeling this strong desire, the *Yakinni* cried to the woman bathing, " O my niece ! may I take care of the baby a little while ? " The mother consented. The *Yakinni* at once seized the child and ran away with him. The mother sprang out of the tank and ran after the fiend, screaming and lamenting. While this hubbub went on, they approached the Pandit's hall.

Now, in those days, BUDDHA was on the earth in his birth as a great Pandit, and he was in the habit of walking in his hall, and hearing and deciding cases brought before him. The two disputants with the child appeared before him. He heard all that each had to say ; each vehemently declared the child to be her own. Then the Pandit drew a line on the floor, placed the mother on one side and the *Yakinni* on the other, and said to the former, " Hold the child by the legs," and to the latter, " Hold him by the arms ; then each of you pull as hard as you can ; and the first that pulls the child over the line shall be adjudged the mother."

The *Yakinni* was rejoiced at this ; for her strength was more than human, and she prepared to pull furiously. But the mother seeing that if she pulled the child at all, he must suffer great pain, fell a-weeping, and said, " No, no ! let her take the child ! I cannot bear to see him hurt ! "

Then said the Pandit to the bystanders, " She who has compassion on her child is the mother. Give the child to her." And all the bystanders rent the air with acclamations at the wisdom of the Teacher, who, turning to the *Yakinni*, said, " As for thee, O vile and culpable one ! I knew thou wast a *Yakinni* ; for thine eyes are red as the olinda seed, and do not twinkle ! Go, but amend thy ways, lest a heavy after-fortune await thee." Thus did the Pandit exhibit his wisdom.

THE TUMPANA FOOL.

There is a part of the country near Kandy called Tumpana, the people of which are not very bright or clever. One of the hamlets thereabouts suffered much from want of water, the soil being dry and the wells few. Once upon a time a man of the hamlet started on a journey into the jungle one morning. About noon he was seen running homeward in a state of great excitement. He called to his neighbours to bring spades and hoes, and go with him, as he had discovered a fine spring in the forest, and wished without loss of time to have it dug up and brought bodily to the village, which would thus, he argued, never suffer from drought any more!

Compare with this the English stories of the men of Gotham and the villagers of Borrowdale. A story almost precisely the same is, MR CAMPBELL of Islay informs the writer, current in the Highlands, being told of men of Assynt. All Aryan races appear to take delight in telling tales of the folks of Daftland.

THE GOLDEN PUMPKIN.

If brass passes for gold, a monkey may pass for a child. There was once a man who had a large piece of gold fashioned in the shape of a pumpkin. It was beautiful to look at, and very precious. He left it in charge of a friend, and went away on a journey. When he came back, the friend gave him a brass pumpkin of the same size and shape as the other, saying that the gold had turned into brass! The owner, being a man of few words and much sense, said nothing, but took the brass pumpkin and went his way. Some days passed over, and as he showed no resentment, the two appeared as friendly as ever. But the owner of the pumpkin had a scheme in his head all the time; he went to the house of his friend when the latter was away, took his child, hid him in the jungle, and came back bringing a monkey. When the father, in great distress, begged and prayed to have his child back, the other said, "Nay, nay; as my gold was turned into brass, your boy has become a monkey, and here he is!" Nor did he restore the child till the golden pumpkin had been restored to him. Ever after that, his friend held him in much greater esteem and respect than he did before!

THE FAITHFUL MONGOOSE.*

Whatever you do, do it thoughtfully. Want of thought works all manner of mischief. The story of the faithful mongoose shows this. The mongoose hates venomous snakes, and always tries to kill them. A poor woman had a tame mongoose who watched her child when she was out of doors, and would not let any mischievous reptile come near or hurt it. One day a snake came into the house and was about to attack the child. The mongoose fell upon the intruder, and after a long fight destroyed it. Some drops of

* The mongoose is the Indian ichneumon. It is easily tamed.

blood fell on, and discoloured, the mongoose's coat. By and by the mother came in, and not seeing her child, but noticing the marks of blood on the mongoose, jumped to the conclusion that the faithful creature had killed her child. Without further parley she slew the mongoose, who, far from harming, had saved the infant's life. Such and so fatal is want of thought.

This, it will be seen, is the counterpart of the pathetic Welsh story of Llewelyn and his faithful hound, Gelert:—

> " Vain, vain was all Llewelyn's woe:
> ' Best of thy kind, adieu !
> The frantic blow which laid thee low
> This heart shall ever rue !'
>
> And now a gallant tomb they raise,
> With costly sculpture decked ;
> And marbles storied with his praise
> Poor Gelert's bones protect.
>
> There never could the spearman pass,
> Or forester unmoved ;
> There oft the tear-besprinkled grass
> Llewelyn's sorrow proved.
>
> And there he hung his horn and spear,
> And there, as evening fell,
> In fancy's ear he oft would hear
> Poor Gelert's dying yell.
>
> And till great Snowdon's rocks grow old,
> And cease the storm to brave,
> The consecrated spot shall hold
> The name of *Gelert's Grave.*"

THE WILY CRANE OUTWITTED.

A wily crane came to a pond which was nearly dried up, and persuaded the fish in it that if they would trust themselves to him, he would carry them one by one in his mouth to another pond where they would find plenty of water and food. They had no choice, and gladly accepted the offer. The crane took them one by one, and had a hearty meal off each. When all had been dispatched, he found a biggish crab in fine toothsome condition (for it was at the proper change of the moon) in the pond, and said to him in the most courteous way, " Now, my friend, I am ready to take you to the other pond, if you will allow me ?" " O sir," replied the crab, "I shall be very glad of your help, but the only way to take me safely and comfortably for both of us is to let me hold on by your neck." The crane agreed, and flew off with his burden. He went near the other pond, lighted on a tree and began meditatively to make arrangements to feast on his passenger. But the crab was too much for him ; for he clung to the crane's neck as tightly as possible, and choked the bird outright ! Then when the crane fell down dead, the crab crept away at his leisure to the water. If you plot destruction to others, the self-same destruction may, very likely, fall upon yourselves.

THE COBRA AND POLANGA.

There are many kinds of serpents, some of noble and generous natures ; but the Nāya (cobra) is the noblest of all. He is benign to mankind, fond of music, readily susceptible to kindness. Indeed, there is, people say, a cobra-world with a king and many grandees and commoners, all cobras. Now, while the cobra is the most princely, the polanga is the meanest and vilest of snakes. These two serpents are at constant feud. How the feud began was on this wise.

One very dry year, when little rain fell, when rivers had dwindled into a slender thread, when tanks were baked hard and brown, and wells and watercourses were dried up, a polanga, suffering agonies from thirst and faint from the overpowering heat, met a cobra looking very lively and refreshed.

"Have you found water anywhere?" gasped the polanga. The other said yes. "Where? O where is it? Tell me, I implore you; for I am dying of thirst!" said the polanga. The cobra replied, "I cannot tell you unless you promise to do no harm to any living thing that may be beside the water." "As for that," answered the polanga, "I will promise anything, so that I may quench this horrible thirst." And he gave a solemn promise. "Well then," said the cobra, "beyond those bushes is a large earthen pan of water in which a child is playing. Go and drink from it, but at your peril do not harm the child!" So saying, they parted. The cobra, after going a little way, began to distrust the polanga, knowing the latter's treacherous disposition and rugged temper, and turned to follow him. He arrived too late ; the polanga had not only drunk of the water, but crept into the pan, where the child began to play with him. On this he grew violently angry, bit the child with all his force, so savagely indeed, that the infant died in a few minutes. The cobra, in hot and fiery indignation, attacked the polanga, and punished him severely, biting off a piece of his tail. Hence to this day all polangas have blunt tails. Ever since, cobras and polangas have been at deadly feud. They are the most venomous of all serpents in Ceylon. When people hate each other mortally, they are said proverbially to be *like cobra and polanga.*

CUTTING OFF ONE'S NOSE TO SPITE AN ENEMY.

It is a common notion that to meet a noseless man when setting out on a journey is an unlucky omen. Two men were enemies. One of the two was about to go on a journey; the other, determined to spite him, cut off his own nose, hid himself on the way, and when the first came up, rushed out, and so disconcerted him that he went home again. Thus, in order to effect a trifling object—for no further ill happened that I have heard of beyond the delay of one day—a feeling of bitter feud caused a man to mutilate himself! From this has sprung the proverbial saying, " *To cut off one's nose to spite an enemy.*"

To this may perhaps be traced the origin of the common English saying, " *Cutting off one's nose to spite one's face !* "

THE BRAGGARTS.

A prawn, an eel, and a tortoise, having cool, comfortable quarters in a swamp, began to boast of their several gifts and accomplishments in the presence of a frog. "I," said the prawn, "have twenty accomplishments with which I can easily escape harm when danger comes near me." "And I," observed the eel, "have ten." "Though not so highly gifted as you two," said the tortoise, "I can reckon on five." The poor frog, who was of a modest, unassuming nature, heard them sing their several praises, and said, as they seemed to expect him to speak, "For my part, I do not think I have more than one, and that is not much to be depended on." While the others were sneering at the frog's horrible want of self-respect, a fisherman came to the spot, thrust down his wicker-basket, and caught all the four. He put in

hand, and seizing the prawn, broke his neck without more ado.
The eel's turn came next; and he was spitted and hung to a branch,
where he soon died. The tortoise was for sport turned on his
back on the dry ground, where he could neither move nor rise, and
became a sight both pitiable and laughable. But the frog, when the
fisherman put his hand near him, used his one accomplishment,
and gave an astonishing spring, by which he nimbly cleared the
basket and got safely away!

Boasters can do little when a real emergency occurs; but the
modest man is often better than his word. At the same time, a
moderate amount of self-conceit is by no means a bad thing.

THE QUEEN AND THE JACKAL.

Never throw away a substance for a shadow, or barter what you
have for something worthless.

There was a King whose Queen thought more of the King of a
neighbouring country than of her own husband. War broke out;
and the two Kings were to decide the matter by single combat.
While they were fighting, the Queen was asked by her husband
to fetch him another sword. She did so, but handed it to his
adversary, giving her husband only the scabbard. This settled the
affair at once, as the latter was immediately killed. Then the
victor took possession of the kingdom and the Queen, and led her
away, nothing loth, with all her jewels and great spoil. They came
to the banks of a river, and there the King, finding the Queen's
society tiresome, stripped her of all her jewels and deserted her.
She lay down beneath the trees, forlorn and disconsolate. As she
. ., a jackal came up, carrying in his mouth a fine piece of meat.
On approaching the stream he spied a dead fish in the water. He
dropped the meat on the bank, and jumped into the river to seize
the fish. While he was in the water, an eagle swooped down on
the meat and bore it away. Thus the jackal, on coming out of the
river, lost the meat, and had but a sorry dead fish for his pains! The
Queen, though in great misery, could not refrain from laughing at
the rueful look of the jackal, and said, "Aha! master jackal, you
have made a poor bargain in sacrificing a noble joint for that
dainty morsel of fish!" "It is very true, O Queen!" replied the
jackal, with great politeness; "but, if it please your majesty, I err

in good company, for the self-same folly I have committed you have been guilty of in a still more deplorable degree ! "

This is curious as grafting the original fable of the Dog and Shadow on another story.

THE RAT AND THE GARANDIYĀ.

If a common danger assails you and your enemies, it is good policy to patch up a truce with them to escape destruction. Then you can outwit them afterwards when more favourable times arrive.

The garandiyā, or rat-snake, hunts rats mercilessly, chasing them over roofs, into holes and crannies, and devouring them greedily when caught. Once on a time, a man caught a garandiyā and a rat, and put them both in a chatty, securing the vessel with a seven-fold cover of cloth, tightly corded. The snake, finding who his fellow-captive was, made ready to eat him, whereupon the rat said, " You can eat me if you like, my lord ; but when you have done so you will still be a prisoner, and will probably die of hunger. But I have a plan that will, if you approve of it and condescend to try it, set you free ; and then you can eat me at your leisure. All you have to do is to raise me up to the cloth on your head. I shall nibble through the cloth, after which your exit will be easy." The garandiyā was struck with the rat's good sense and ingenuity, and raised him up. The rat bit a hole in the first fold of cloth, and got between it and the second. He then went a few inches off and bit through the second, and so on through each of the folds in succession. But he took good care not to make a hole straight through all the folds. Thus he escaped with ease and great peace of mind, while the garandiyā found himself unable to get out, as the holes in the different folds were so far apart.

THE CRANES, THE COBRA, AND THE MONGOOSE.

A family of cranes lived up a hollow tree. There they built their nests, brought up their young, and on the whole led a happy life. They would, indeed, have been quite at their ease, if a cobra had not taken up his abode in an ant-hill at the foot of the tree, and every now and then climbed up and ate a few of the eggs. This was not to be borne. The cranes, however, not daring to attack the cobra themselves, schemed to enlist on their side a mongoose, who is a sworn enemy of venomous snakes. The mongoose lived some way off ; and, that he might not lose his way, the cranes laid a trail of small fish from the jungle where he mostly stayed, up to the ant-hill, hoping that when he reached the ant-hill and saw the cobra, he would, as is his custom, pounce upon the snake and do him to death. Everything fell out to a marvel up to a certain point. The mongoose saw the fish, ate, and tracked his way up to the ant-hill. But when he reached it, he looked up and saw the young and plump, but helpless, cranes in the tree. In an instant he rushed up the tree, and killed and ate the young cranes as fast as he could, nor did he rest till he had killed them all ! When we scheme for vengeance we should remember that it may fall on others besides those it is intended for.

It is worth noting how often cobras figure in Sinhalese stories, and how respectfully they are dealt with. This is significant of the old snake-worship once prevalent in the island, traces of which still linger, and will probably long continue to do so.

HOW TO OUTWIT A THIEF.

There was once a villager, the expertest thief that ever was known, so clever in stealing and disposing of the things he took— in the which, by the way, he had the help of his wife—that, though often suspected, he was never found out. But the wariest are caught at last ; and so it proved with him. After many years of plunder, he stole a box of jewels. The owner complained to the judge, and named whom he suspected. There was, however, no evidence to bring the charge home to the thief. Then the judge said, " Go home, keep quiet for a while, and, after that, bring a suit against the thief to recover from him the white bullock which every-body knows to be his." Now, this white bullock was undeniably the thief's own ; and it was, moreover, a great favourite with both the thief and his wife. The suit was duly instituted, and on the day fixed came on for hearing. The bullock was brought to the court, and the parties were in attendance, each with his crowd of witnesses, ready to swear anything and everything at a moment's warn-ing ! The case being called, and plaintiff and defendant ap-pearing in the court, the judge privately called a messenger and said to him, " Go at once to the house of the defendant (the thief), call his wife aside, and tell her that her husband has sent you with a message to the effect that the suit about the bullock is going on, that the judge appears very unfavourable, and that she is to send by you the case of jewels she knows of, in order to bribe the judge with the contents, and so obtain undisputed possession of the favourite bullock!" The messenger started, delivered the message to the thief's wife, who fell at once into the trap, and gave up the case of jewels. When they were brought into court, they were identified as the property of the plaintiff, and were there and then restored to him, while the thief was summarily convicted, and received a severe and condign measure of punishment.

CUNNING BEATS STRENGTH.

Cunning is better than strength. A lion and a tortoise lived as neighbours by the banks of a river which was deep, slow-flowing, and muddy. They were on very friendly terms, and often talked together. One day they laid a heavy wager as to which of them could cross the river the sooner—the lion by leaping, the tortoise by diving, and swimming under the water. Now, one tortoise is very much like another; and the one who laid the wager with the lion concerted with another tortoise, one of his own kith and kin, that, immediately on the signal being given for the lion to spring and his opponent to dive, the latter's confederate should pop his head out of the water at the farther side! As it was schemed, so was it carried out; and the tortoise triumphantly won the wager.

Old-world household stories are very plentiful in CEYLON. The foregoing may be of interest as showing how rich a field, one little harvested yet, lies open to the gleaner. When it is remembered that, besides the aboriginal wild race, the Veddahs, the Island is the home of Sinhalese, an Aryan race from the upper valley of the Ganges, of Tamils, of Moors, the descendants of the ancient Arab navigators who, as SINBAD avouches, voyaged often to Serendib, of Malays, not to mention Parsīs, Chinese, Kaffirs from Eastern Africa, Maldivians, Bengalis, and many others, men of widely diverse descent and creeds, the abundance of, so to speak, unwrought folk-lore will be readily recognised.

It is the writer's hope, should the present venture meet with favour and acceptance, to offer a larger and more varied selection to the reader hereafter.

R.

Sinhalese and Pāli Poems,

ADDRESSED TO H.R.H. THE DUKE OF EDINBURGH.

A PLACE may, perhaps, not inappropriately be found here for the
subjoined, as illustrative of Sinhalese and Pāli poetry of the most
recent date. They are renderings of addresses in those languages
presented to the DUKE OF EDINBURGH by the native Chiefs of the
Southern Province of Ceylon, in March 1870. The originals were
the composition of three learned native scholars chosen by the Chiefs
for the purpose. The first stanza of the Sinhalese poem, after a
fashion dear to pandits of the country, is so constructed in the
original as to be capable of two distinct renderings, each of which
is sought to be given in the English version.

THE SINHALESE ADDRESS.

I.

Long live the QUEEN OF ENGLAND! the pure of heart, revered,
A blessing to Her people still, to all mankind endeared!
Her throne is set in ENGLAND, that world-ensheltering shore,
The chosen home of Learning, which waxes ever more!

Or,

All hail the pure, bright LAKSHMI, who sprang from ocean's foam,
High VISHNU's bride, who rules supreme o'er every royal home!
Hers is the thready lotus, with countless petals rare,
The chosen seat of BRAHMA, which makes the waters fair!

II.

May He be victor ever, the graceful and serene,
Royal, illustrious as a gem, the well-loved of our QUEEN,
Who graces well Her ancient throne, and fills the earth with fame,
And wins the hearts of all who do meet homage to Her name!

III.

Of all the many realms that own our SOVRAN LADY's sway,
The LADY of the English land resplendent as the day,
A land for power and wealth renowned—among these mighty lands,
Far, far away is LANKA's Isle, of small account it stands!

IV.

Few are the folk within its shores, we Eastern folk who dwell ;
And marvellous it is to us that we are loved so well
As thus to have the joy to see our LADY'S well-loved Son !
By this we know our QUEEN regards with favour every one :

V.

Of all Her realms, or great or small ! For, seeing we are all
Right loyal to Her throne and laws whatever may befall,
Our SOVEREIGN sends Her SON to us, an earnest of Her care !
How shall we then in fitting phrase our joy and thanks declare ?

VI.

May She who, with a mother's love, has deigned so high a grace
The ruler of so vast a realm, the friend of every race,
Who loves and guards the grateful hearts intrusted to Her will,
Find every wish Her soul desires accomplished for her still !

VII.

O high-born PRINCE and well beloved ! whose presence brings delight,
As floods the autumn moon the sea with happy radiance bright !
Live long, and precious as the eye, so men may of Thee deem !
And never once come sorrow nigh, not even in a dream !

THE PĀLI ADDRESS.

I.

Long live the QUEEN OF ENGLAND Her wide domain to guard !
Thoughtful and far-renowned is She, and all who own her ward
Revere Her, as the crescent moon is worshipped by her train !
Kings and great nations honour Her ! All-glorious is Her reign !

II.

Like darting flames Her glory spreads to realms beyond the seas,
Subduing every foe, as fire lays low the forest trees !
Her mercy, like the pure, cold stream that from Gangutri flows,
Refreshes all Her lieges' hearts, and gives them glad repose !

III.

CEYLON is but a little Isle, the imperial garment's hem ;
Few are its folk, and little heed the world bestows on them !
Yet, filled with love and thought for us, though few and far away,
Our SOVEREIGN LADY sends Her SON to grace our shores this day !

IV.

Wise is the far-descended PRINCE, whom men admire and praise,
And graced with many a noble gift : so doth He greet our gaze !
He sees with joy the festal shows the loyal throngs prepare ;
And takes our eyes and hearts in thrall ! Such is His presence rare !

V.

Like the young orb that mounting gives rare promise for the day,
Rejoicing hearts as lotus-blooms the sunbeam's earliest ray,
Grief He dispels, as dawn the dew, as night when morn comes on !
And men for him don gay attire, as peacocks greet the sun!

VI.

To INDIA's vast palatial realm our Isle is but the key :
Yet beautiful exceedingly—and well assured are we
Its rare and radiant loveliness delights our ROYAL GUEST,
Who with sweet words and gracious ways has gladdened every breast.

VII.

O well-loved PRINCE ! as through the Isle in state You journey on,
May You the lieges cheer, as cheer the lotus-blooms the swan !
Dispelling grief as weariness the fragrant breeze o'erpowers,
And glad the learned and the good, as moonlight glads the flowers !

VIII.

From far and near the lieges come to greet their MONARCH's SON :
With honeyed words He fills their ears, delighting every one !
May He their wants and wishes learn, and graciously bestow
Counsel and aid on all who seek our Island's state to know !

[In the eighth stanza, the first and the last letters, in the original
Pāli, when taken together, form the sentence DĪPĒ LŌKAN
SŌCHE TETU, which means, "MAY HE NOT FORGET THE PEOPLE
OF THIS ISLAND!"

After the foregoing, follows a farewell stanza, which may be
freely rendered into English thus] :—

Farewell ! Farewell ! Rejoicing go where Fame and Fortune guide !
Long life and health and strength be yours, whatever may betide !
The Royal House is as a chain with rarest pearls beset,
And You, a priceless pearl, O PRINCE, we never shall forget!

PRINTED BY BALLANTYNE AND COMPANY
EDINBURGH AND LONDON

www.ingramcontent.com/pod-product-compliance
Lightning Source LLC
Chambersburg PA
CBHW060614030726
47498CB00005B/1675